The Genius
of Hunger

The Genius of Hunger

short stories
Diane Goodman

Carnegie Mellon University Press
Pittsburgh 2002

A
FIC

Book design: Sean Mintus
Cover design: James Mojonnier

Library of Congress Control Number: 2002091185
ISBN: 0-88748-360-7

10 9 8 7 6 5 4 3 2 1

For Suzanne Lois Goodman
1931 - 1971

And having found them once
You were sure to find them again.
Someone had always been there
Though you were always alone.

Seamus Heaney, The Plantation

~ Stories ~

Joan

One's sympathies, of course, were all on the side of life. Also, when there was nobody to care or to know, this gigantic effort on the part of an insignificant little moth, against a power of such magnitude, to retain what no one else valued or desired to keep, moved one strangely.

Virginia Woolf, The Death of the Moth

When Joan approached 10th Street, the turn into the Wild Oates Supermarket, the light turned red and she stopped. Behind her, a blonde haired girl in a convertible with New York plates slammed on her brakes and from the rear-view mirror, Joan could see the girl mouthing curses. Ignore her, Joan admonished herself, and then tried to be discreet about moving her nose toward her armpits; although she wasn't sure what she could do if there was the odor she suspected, she was compelled to know.

There was. Her eyes shot up to meet the movement in her peripheral vision, the driver in the car next to her moving behind the tinted window glass. The shape seemed male: did he see what she just did? God, he could be a colleague, a person she'd met at a book signing, a parent of one of her son's friends from school. Her face began to warm.

And then the car behind her honked its horn because the light had turned green. Joan put her blinker on, an action that seemed to ignite the horn into one continuous surge.

Very few ordinary things were easy for Joan. Miami was famous for irate and irrational drivers who generally ignored each other but when this girl behind her displayed rage at discovering she was going to turn, Joan felt the familiar shame of having done something stupid. She inched up under light, checking her rear view mirror in spasmodic bursts: the girl, who appeared to be beautiful behind black sunglasses, was banging her fists against her steering wheel and throwing her hair around in disgust; fi-

11

nally, there was a second free from traffic and Joan turned. The girl nearly clipped her as she sped by.

The parking lot was packed but when Joan finally spotted a row not completely full, she let out a sigh of relief. Joan had grown up in Miami but she had never been able to assume the self-importance of the strays that after even only a couple of months, confidently called it home. Driving nearly always held the promise of trauma for Joan. In the Wild Oates parking lot, she eventually rested in an empty space.

Joan's wallet was in the glove compartment and she took fifty dollars out and then replaced the wallet; she did not want to be tempted to overspend. She would just get something to fix for dinner tonight, and maybe a treat for her and Howard to have while they watched the late night news.

Joan stepped out of her old Honda into the steam bath that didn't seem to affect other people, skinny people. All around her, girls and women and boys and men and children and old people were running errands, meeting friends, heading toward home and they all appeared miraculously cool. Joan wore suits and hose to work no matter what the temperature—hose that practically disintegrated from sweat when she peeled them off at night. I could, she thought, melt into this asphalt. She tried to hurry toward the store entrance.

In the store, the aisles were very narrow; people bumped carts and each other as a matter of course. But the organic produce was fresh and the variety of specialty items too tempting to bypass this store and shop exclusively at the big, wide, modern Publix. Joan was almost at the door, still worrying that her body odor was noticeable, that the thin aisles would put her too close to other shoppers. Just before she got into the store, she lifted her arms like a bird considering flight, hoping that this last blast of heavy breeze would suck some of the smell away.

A rush of very cold air and then the beautiful hand-printed signs for produce and nuts and wine everywhere; the coffee, the cereals, the gleaming berries, the bulk bins of baking ingredients froze Joan in the entrance; she took a deep breath of the deliciously frigid air.

"Lady? Come in or go out, ok?" This from a young boy stocking boxes of giant blueberries.

"Sorry," Joan said from under a weak smile. She rarely allowed herself trips to Wild Oates and she looked forward to them like vacations. Everything was too expensive but she loved the rights of perusal, examination, comparison, selection, satisfaction. She would smell exotic fruits and Jamaican coffee beans, hand-pick wheat berries for bread and buy imported jams. She would not let these rude impatient strangers spoil her mood.

In the produce section, Joan lingered. Being a chubby woman who delayed buying clothes that fit because she was always certain she would lose the extra fifteen pounds she carried around her middle, Joan felt comfortable in Produce. Everyone had to eat and buying fresh vegetables was acceptable for even the fattest of middle-aged women. She was a wife and the mother of a growing teenage boy: she had to shop. Joan chose mandarin oranges, bok choy, scallions, grape tomatoes, porcini mushrooms and tiny new potatoes; she would make a vegetarian stir fry tonight. Howard would eat anything she fixed; he was always pleased with her. Joan knew lots of other women who complained relentlessly about their cheating, ignoring, sleeping, partying husbands and she felt lucky. Richie would complain about everything she fixed but as long as she thought it healthful and tasty, she was able to bypass his adolescent complaints. She scooped half a pound of unsalted peanuts into a bag, thinking she would roast them in soy sauce, sprinkle them on top of the stir fry.

At the end of the produce section was the wine. Joan loved wine. She loved the labels—Napa, Sonoma, France, Italy, Australia; she loved to match wines with her recipes and to add them to her cooking. Wild Oates always had great deals on good wine: today there was a Kenwood Chardonnay for $9.99—unheard of—and an Arrowood Merlot for $29.00, for which she splurged. She rounded the corner to the cheese and olive section, feeling energized and anonymous and looking forward to getting home to cook.

A mundane cheddar for Richie would at least put a temporary halt to his phrase, "there's never anything to eat in this house" but Joan also, reluctantly, was lifting a full-crème brie when she heard someone call her name. Before turning around, before being sure who was standing behind her, she felt her free hand mechanically go to her stomach where a roll of fat was settled over the waistband of her skirt. Looking down, she saw what she expected to see and she knew when she turned around, Juanita Pedrosa would be able to see them, too: pale ample parentheses of fat between every button of her too-tight button-down blouse, where the fabric strained and opened. But she had to turn, focusing on her arms, keeping them close to her sides.

"Chica," Juanita said, leaning toward Joan for a hug that Joan—with her arms bolted to her hips—tried to prevent, "it's been ages." Joan then placed one arm on Juanita's bare shoulder and with the other, tossed the brie backward, hoping it made it into the case.

"But I saw you yesterday when you dropped Alvaro off," she said. Alvaro Pedrosa and Richie had grown up together and the mothers often chauffeured the two boys around, Juanita in her Range Rover and Joan in on of her series of used Hondas.

"Oh? I didn't realize you were home." Joan was lying. Yesterday, when Richie showed up unexpectedly with an urgent demand that Joan take Alvaro home, Joan had been working at her computer and was wearing Howard's old sweat pants and a t-shirt that was too tight: she was not about to hop out of her car and greet the impeccable Juanita Pedrosa. So when Alvaro jumped out of the Honda at the same time Juanita came out of the house, Joan had pretended as if she didn't see her and backed out of their driveway too fast.

"Lame, Mom" Richie had said.

"What, Rich?"

"The way you blew off Mrs. Pedrosa. Don't you like

14

her?"

"What are you talking about, honey? I didn't even see her."

"Oh, Mom: Come *on.*"

But her she was, wearing a tiny powder-blue sundress with matching sandals and her trademark designer sunglasses on top of her full head of cropped black hair. Joan lifted one warm arm and tried to stick some damp errant strands of her own light brown hair back into her bun. Juanita also had only one child, but he was a confident muscular athlete; she also had a size 4 figure, flawless skin and a grating nearly falsetto voice. Joan smiled.

"So how are you," Juanita asked, "how is work?" Juanita didn't work so the question always seemed condescending. Joan sucked in her stomach and some air to respond; when she did, she realized that her bladder was full.

"Good. I just finished editing an art catalogue. And I'm going to Boston on Thursday to give a talk on antique silver. Oh, and Richard is leaving Thursday also to go to golf camp," Joan said, in a rush of fake enthusiasm. Just then, Joan became aware that a woman was trying to get around her to get to the olives but she was afraid to move much closer to Juanita; the woman interested in olives moved to Joan's side and with her hip, nudged her aside.

Immediately, Joan's throat tensed with righteous fury, the kind she always felt and wished she could sustain: but just as swiftly, the rage was replaced by a more familiar hollow of embarrassment: "Sorry," was all Joan could manage to say to the woman who had used her own body to move Joan's out of her way.

Oblivious to this exchange, Juanita said, "Oh, yes, Richie is off to camp. Too bad—Alvie wanted him to come for the weekend to Eleuthra with us."

Joan wanted to disappear. Actually, she wanted to cold cock Juanita and step over her on the way to the rice and pasta aisle; instead, she nodded her head and became even more aware of the moisture beneath her armpits growing; she had told Richie he could not go with the Pedrosas to the Bahamas but she had refused to give a reason why. That same night, she had also forced him to eat an egg-white omelet with wheat germ, raisins and soy-based "sausage" that she had read about in a health-food magazine.

"I hate you," Richie had said, after choking down the last bite, leaving a pile of fresh under-cooked peas Joan had thought she'd steamed through.

" Well, I love you," Joan had answered brightly so as not to cause an explosion and Howard had nodded at her, smiling.

"You're ruining my life. No one plays golf, Mom; no one my age. And the Pedrosas have a pool on the ocean at Eleuthra. And jet skis."

But Richie was as good at golf as he was ever going to get at a sport and Joan knew she knew best. She had never been good at disciplining Richie; she was very good at calming young petulant painters whose work she reviewed and who had not yet earned their enormous egos, and she was confident when dealing with irate agents, yawning audiences, exasperatingly difficult interviewees, her manipulative mother-in-law. But when it came to her only child, Joan often did not know what was the right thing to say. When Richie spoke to her with such obvious contempt, which was more often than she could bear to admit, he rendered her powerless to do anything but try to appease him. The meaner and more disrespectful he became, the more gentle she became. Richie was everything: she wanted everything for him and worked on extra books, went on dull lecture tours—anything—so that he could have what all the rich kids he went to school with had. Richie could never understand the sacrifices she made to protect him from envy; all he knew was that she forced him to do things he didn't want to and prevented him from participating in activities he craved: skiing was dangerous, jet-skiing worse. When she brought his breakfast to the table in the mornings, she saw him disapprove of her flannel nightgown or, if she was going to work, her outdated discount suits and knew he was thinking she wasn't as fit or as pretty as his friends' moms. His sneer broke her heart but she couldn't raise any anger. Why should she be mad? Kids said and did all sorts of things they didn't mean or didn't understand or didn't understand the implications of, she told herself, and certainly Richie fit into all of those categories; but the night Joan refused to let Richie go with the Pedrosas and he fled the dining room calling her a bitch under his breath, she noticed that when she said goodnight to Howard, after he had kissed her on both temples and lightly squeezed her breasts as he had done every night for twenty years, she felt like crying.

"Yes, he wanted to go with you all to Eleuthra but he wanted to golf, too, and you know, he just couldn't do both."

"I understand" Juanita said, with such genuine understanding that Joan wondered if Juanita had been inside her own mind and knew the truth. "Still, even if the boys can't get together, we can: let's have lunch."

Oh, lunch. The idea of sitting across from Juanita at her club on Fisher Island, flicking her glance from the menu (broiled grouper) to Juanita's unbelievably flat belly to the menu (Fettuccine Alfredo with Lobster and Cream) to Juanita's finger pointing to the Caesar Salad. Then when the salad came, with dressing on the side, Juanita would say, "Joan, would like to try this?" which Joan would hear as "Joan, you ought to be having this" and Joan would have to fight the urge to respond, "Why on earth would I want to eat a bowl of dry lettuce?"

"Lunch sounds great but I really can't make any plans until I've plotted out my next project. I'll call."

"Good. Love to Rich. And to Howard. Ciao, dear" and they kissed as friends and acquaintances and strangers do in Miami and went their separate ways.

Baked tortilla chips flavored with lime; yogurt and green onion potato chips somehow produced with 50% less fat; veggie spirals—translucent pastel curls of snack made with tomatoes, green peppers, jalapeno chilies. Free of Juanita, Joan resumed her reading ritual—which snacks were the most authentically healthy? Which ones would Richie actually eat, actually be happy eating and force a smile from her son? Juanita's cart had been filled with healthy junk food for her family and as Joan tried to resist the urge to choose the snacks she herself would most like, she knew that either Juanita never had a single craving for any of it, or that she ate with abandon because she could.

"Darn," she said aloud, unsure whether the irritation was directed to Juanita or herself. Juanita had done nothing but live off her successful husband, off the glories of her handsome athletic son. Joan, on the other hand, had edited seventeen art history books, written two herself, and consulted on hundreds more but was forever having to tell people who she was and what she did. And Richie, unlike Alvie Pedrosa, was slight and not athletically gifted. He was smart, though; his teachers wrote or called her with glowing reports of his mastery with languages, his computer skills, the passionate way he played the piano. Richie had won more academic awards than any student in his class and Joan was extraordinarily proud. Yet when she witnessed how angry and unhappy he was, she tried to tell him that in the future, brains counted so much more than brawn. Intellectual prowess so out-weighed good cheeks, good shoulders, good skin, the ability to throw a football or dunk a basket. Joan believed this but she knew Richie didn't; all Richie could see was what was right in front of him—the glory of sports, good looks, vacations in the Bahamas.

"Lady? Could you move?" In the thin aisle, a casual boy slightly older than Richie was trying to get his cart past her. He was clearly impatient; he tried to push his cart and it hit her right hip. Then he backed it up and tried it again, but it hit her again, this time closer to her full bladder. He sighed loudly and shook his head; then he gestured with his chin for her to move out of his way. The embarrassment made Joan panic: the aisle was narrow but she was not ready to leave it yet: she still hadn't picked out a snack for Richie. But she wasn't sure how to maneuver her cart. There was an old woman just making her way past them, moving her cart slowly but with purpose and, thankfully, with success. But at that moment, the space between Joan, this boy and that woman was virtually non-existent. The boy was making her nervous; the possibility of an angry outburst loomed. Joan had been on the other end of too many young rash snotty kids in drug stores, movie theatres, the library: they thought they were special because they had good looks and good bodies and played sports. This boy had a hard body and no patience. She had also been on the other end of countless irrational outbursts at home: Richie yelled at her without warning; if she spent all of her time trying to avoid his anger, she still wouldn't be able to predict what made him lash out at her.

"Lady, I need to get by you, ok? You're taking up the whole aisle."

Was she taking up the whole aisle? Joan looked into his face, crinkled with annoyance and saw what he saw: a dumpy, sweaty, middle-aged woman lasciviously contemplating food she shouldn't eat.

"I have a teenage son," she offered.

"So what?" he said. "I have to go, man."

Whether he liked it or not, Richie would balk at her choice of snacks once he saw her pull them from a Wild Oates bag. He wouldn't eat them out of principle. But she would, and her aged suits from Burdines would stretch tighter across her ass. So she quickly chose a package of barbequed corn chips and prepared to move on.

"Oh. Sorry," Joan said and she felt sorry though she wasn't sure for what, and just as quickly as the apology flew out, she went to move her cart so she could move herself. But when she did, she inadvertently shoved the cart and in the process, it toppled a display of organic rice cakes.

"Oh, great," the kid said, with terrific disdain, and Joan looked down at a few dozen packages of health snacks that had tumbled into the narrow aisle between them. Now this boy—whose cart contained soy milk, two salmon filets, a small piece of the full-crème brie, some organic vegetable crackers, and a large bunch of beautiful purple grapes—was stuck between her and a mess of plastic-wrapped rice cakes. He shoved her cart diagonally into the shelf with his own and moved on, shaking his head.

"Oh, it's nothing," Joan said, "I'll just pick them up." She had to move herself gingerly between her cart and the mess she'd made; but she felt relieved when she bent down to pick up the packages, because now the boy was gone. When both hands were full of columns of rice cakes, she began to stand up hoping no one else had seen her, and that was when simultaneously she heard her skirt tear and felt an unearthly yank in her lower back.

The pain stopped her in the most awkward of positions, somewhere between a half-crawl and an imitation of a crab; for a spilt second, she recalled a childhood game where she was moving around and when someone called out a particular word—she could not remember the word—everyone had to freeze in the position they had just assumed. But now, as an adult in a supermarket, she became terrified when she realized she really could not move: her back felt as though a burning steel plate had been imbedded beneath her vertebrae. All movement stopped: she simply could not stand up.

Bent like an overturned chair, she still had the rice cakes in her arms. Blessedly, no one else was in the aisle at that moment, as Joan forced herself to think hard about what to do. She had never had a pain like this, paralyzing and mesmerizing at once. A balloon of fear began to fill the space in her throat and it occurred to her that she could pass out. She remained bent over at a right angle. Then she swallowed some air, stifled a burp that threatened to escape, and tried extremely slowly to straighten up; a millimeter of movement released a wrenching pain. My God, she thought, what is happening to me? She heard her own voice answer in a whisper: *it doesn't matter: you are in the Wild Oates Mar-*

ket; you have got to move. Focusing on a smaller problem, she lifted her arms and let the packages of rice cakes fall into her cart. Then she placed her hands on the cart's handle and clenched her fists.

A smoking anvil had replaced her lower spine, the pain heavy and solid and burning. When she tried the smallest of movements to straighten up, it became heavier and hotter, so fierce that it held her down and took her breath.

Had she been able to think clearly, she might have anticipated her next problem: someone was coming down the narrow aisle from behind, someone who needed to get past her. "Look, Mom," she heard a small voice say, and in response, "Shhh, Sami." Joan remembered the split in her skirt, though she was unsure exactly where it was or how bad.

"Excuse me," the mother said to Joan, "can we get by?"

If I could move, you could, Joan thought and now she could feel her face darken and moisture forming at her temples. She tried to move to the left and to take the cart with her but every movement was full of fury and her hands were welded to the handle of the cart.

"I can't seem to make this cart move," Joan offered weakly, "I think the wheels are stuck."

"I'll move it," the tiny Sami said, and before anyone could stop her she shoved the cart, with Joan stuck to it, to the side. A blast of pain now flamed up through Joan's entire back and she thought she was going to throw up. She was flush against the Oriental Snacks display and not unaware that one wrong move could cause the entire shelf to come down around her.

"Sorry," Sami's mother said, and then in a whisper very close to Joan's ear, "you know, your skirt is torn in the back."

"Thank you," Joan said softly, fairly sure she saw Sami's mother wince backward from being so close to Joan's armpits which, by now, were completely soaked through and reeking.

The mother and daughter made their way down the aisle and around the corner and when they did, Joan finally took some deep breaths and then turned, excruciatingly slowly, back toward the snack shelves. Joan was becoming delirious with pain but she still possessed enough rationality to recognize that she needed a plan. If she stood in a certain position, the pain crested and then settled, smoldering into the lower portion of her back but its containment allowed her to think. She looked up and could see a small line at the cash register at the end of her aisle. If she could bear the pain long enough, she could lean on the cart and get there; she could pay for her groceries and then take advantage of the Wild Oates carry out service she had never before used. Once in the car, she could call Howard and he would come and help her. Howard would do anything for her though it occurred to her at this exact moment, that she was not sure why.

Now that she had a plan, Joan geared up for the trek. She started by willing her mind away from the slit in her skirt—which she imagined was directly in the middle of her ass—and toward her goal. But try as she might, she could not dismiss the very real possibility that she had not put on underwear beneath her nude colored pantyhose. She also recognized a new fear: the pain in her back was so severe that she could hardly feel her hips and now she wondered if it would eclipse her ability to control her bladder.

Desperate, Joan started to move, but every step released a fireball of pain. She was nauseous and feared throwing up as well as peeing on the floor. Her bun was coming undone in the heat and she could feel her hair tickling her neck and pieces of it sticking to her chin but she dared not move a hand from the cart, lest she literally collapse on the floor in Wild Oates. She took one small step with one foot at a time, like an elderly woman with a walker. Joan had heard people talk about back pain before but she had never really taken them seriously; her uncle had complained of it for years but Joan had always felt he was exaggerating so that her Aunt Rose would wait on him hand and foot. She wondered if she had Advil in her purse.

The trip to the cash register was taking an eternity. In

the midst of it, a woman around her age in a jogging bra and nylon shorts was coming up the aisle fast; when she stopped just in front of Joan to look at brands of Veggie Sticks, she was jogging in place.

This woman's breasts did not move while she hopped up and down but her ponytail bobbed like a cheerleader's. She was breathing in and out methodically and on each exhale repeating to herself the word, "Halt." Yet Joan was inching toward her.

The woman looked over and into Joan's cart. "Are those good?" she asked.

The rice cakes. Joan hadn't even looked in the cart during the time she was trying to figure out how to get the hell out of the store so she had forgotten about the dozen or so packages of rice cakes she'd caused to fall and then dropped into her cart.

"Um, I don't know, exactly," Joan said, "I haven't tried them yet." Joan was trying to think quickly: she had to get those rice cakes out of there before she made it to the register because the fifty dollars she'd taken from her wallet would just cover her produce and wine purchases and she really didn't think she could stand another potential humiliation at Wild Oates. But still, she could not lift her hands from the cart. "Would you like a package?" Joan needed help and this woman was...well, she was there.

"Here," Joan said, "why don't you try one of these? And by the way, I was wondering if you..."

"...Oh, no," the woman nearly shouted, and with emphasis, "those are way too fattening for me," giving Joan the once over. In this kind of pain, Joan could not even attempt to suck her stomach in as she normally did, and so Joan watched this incredibly fit and bouncy woman display her disapproval. And then as if this woman thought Joan had the power to force-feed her a rice cake, she said, "you enjoy," and of she went. Jogging. Somehow then, instead of feeling stupid, Joan rolled her eyes and laughed.

Something very funny, very curious, was happening to

Joan. She was in terrific pain and there was the very real possibility that her bladder might give out on her; her hair was damp with sweat and falling into her ears; her ears, in fact, were dripping with sweat. Dark wet stains were growing on her beige polyester blouse—two below her breasts, one between them, one absorbing the rim of her skirt. Now there was no doubt: a strong animal smell was pumping out of her pores with every heavy breath she took. Although Joan was getting closer to her destination, each time she took a small step the fuming in her back intensified. She had to force herself to keep going at the same time she had to force herself to stifle the sounds rising in her throat. Yet, in the midst of what truly was the greatest panic Joan could remember experiencing, she felt an unerring kind of strength. It almost felt like pride but it was more complicated than that; it was unrecognizable but at the same time dependable. She trusted it. This wicked pain was justifying fat and sweat and bad hair: rising up through the mass of agony came the certainty that with this battle raging in her back, no mistake she could make now mattered. She could faint, vomit, piss on the floor. None of it mattered. Fuck, Joan thought, with an alien clarity. Fuck everybody.

Propelled by the power of legitimate crisis, Joan forced herself to the end of the aisle. When she got there, like a driver at a four way stop, she looked both ways before crossing over to take her place in line. But she did not see the young guy from earlier in the snack aisle come twisting around the corner. So when his cart knocked right into her left side, she could not stop it from dislodging her from her stronghold and sending her down, just in front of a cooler full with bagels and flavored non-dairy cream cheeses.

Joan's head landed on the cooler's rim and the cold air graced her face, which was on fire. Sweat, or possibly blood, was trickling down the back of her neck and sliding under her collar. When she went down, her skirt shot up over the tops of her thighs; one foot was pointing straight ahead but the other was cranked unnaturally west and despite the unrelenting pain in her back, she could only think about what all the people who had stopped and were staring could see: beneath her sweat-soaked pantyhose, she was now absolutely sure she had not put on underpants.

"Jesus, lady," the kid who knocked her down said, "what the hell are you doing?"

This struck Joan as amusing; *I'm trying like hell not to pee on the floor*, she said to herself. Then she shifted, only to realize that she could not move her legs.

"What the hell is your problem?" the kid shouted again. "Are you drunk? Get up, for God's sake" and he tapped the bottom of her foot twice with his own foot. Joan looked up into this boy's face. He was very handsome, Joan noticed, maybe a model. He was wearing soft, faded Levis that came down right to his hips and a dark blue shirt—cotton, with tiny white squares. Around his neck was one of those leather strips with three white beads and they moved against his Adam's apple. Those were the kind of necklaces guys got from their girlfriends; Richie hadn't had a girlfriend yet, Joan acknowledged: having just finished his sophomore year of high school, he still hadn't trespassed the boundary between playing jokes on girls he liked and taking one out for pizza. When Joan mentioned girls to Richie, he usually told her to shut up. The memory made Joan cringe; the cringe returned her to her immediate problem.

"I can't get up," Joan whispered, in the voice she sometimes used to soften Richie's contempt.

"What do you mean you can't get up? Just get up," he repeated and rolled his eyes the way Richie did every time she made a suggestion or a comment or told him he was cute. Joan knew Richie was insecure about his big features, his adolescent acne. She knew he blamed her. He blamed her for his brains, too.

"I can't get up," she said again, but this time louder and more definitively. The clear irrefutable fact of her predicament was fortifying. She imagined that people on their deathbeds probably experienced the kind of freedom that let them say everything they ever wanted to say to anyone before leaving the world. "Something has happened to my back and I cannot get up."

The boy looked at her as if she was speaking Russian.

"You knocked me over," she said, taking advantage of his surprise, "and now you are going to have to help me." Her voice was authoritative but confidently gentle. Despite being splayed out and showing the world of Miami Beach's organic shoppers her crotch, despite being middle-aged and overweight and stinking and not Juanita Pedrosa, Joan understood she possessed a strong but temporary power and she knew she had to use it now.

"Help me up," she stated.

"I can't lift you, man," the kid said, "Just try to get up," and now he tapped her calf a couple of times with his foot. He was wearing clogs and for some reason, this struck Joan as hilarious. It also made her feel real anger.

"Look, Sven," she said, in a voice she had never heard herself use before, "I told you: I cannot get up." By now, a small crowd had gathered around and Joan could see the tops of other heads—cashiers and customers in line—straining to see what was going on. Her breath was coming out fast but she felt surprisingly calm. She could also feel the cold metal of the case against her neck and the pain in her back stretching down into her hips, up toward her abdomen. She was thinking about trying to shift just so she could close her legs when the boy said, "What's the matter with you?" in a whisper, as if he didn't want anyone else to know he was asking.

This was a question, Joan knew, that would take a long time to answer. But one response was inevitable.

"I don't know."

The boy was staring at her so she said it again: "I don't know" and when he still didn't respond she became annoyed and said, "Well, for starters, Sherlock, I can't move." Joan heard the sarcasm in her own voice that she did not intend; it felt good.

Joan had always wanted to talk to someone that way, to give back what she took so often and so passively. She wanted to call someone an asshole, someone who deserved to be called that. A crowd of nosy strangers were pressing in but no one offered to help. She was cold, she was pretty sure her head was bleeding, she had no idea what she could do or who was going to help her and this teenage boy was staring down at her as if this was all her fault, as if she was lying there like that because she was stupid and clumsy instead of because she was seriously hurt. She twisted herself up to speak and was just about to say, "Look asshole," when instead the movement caused a sound an animal might make when it doesn't realize its leg is caught in a steel trap and tries to get away.

The sound that came from Joan produced a look of contempt on the boy's face, a look that might have been infuriating, except that it brought Joan a jolt of recognition. She'd seen it hundreds of times before, this involuntary cover-up for the kind of helpless self-consciousness she encountered everyday. It was a look that inhabited her son's eyes and made his face a fortress against what she now suddenly knew was his natural instinct to love her. So precariously did Richie straddle the line between contempt and compassion. How like Richie this young boy was at this moment—shuffling, jerking his head around, knowing he needed to help her but not knowing how to, wanting her just to make his bad behavior better and then go away. It was the fear of not knowing what to do that prevented Richie and this boy from being kind and presented Joan with the knowledge of exactly what she needed to do.

"Look," she said, with the nervous brightness and complicit understanding she was used to and now believed must have had some impact on her son, "I know this is a very awkward situation for you, for us both, but," and here she let out a small laugh, "do you think you could help me?"

The boy stood straight up, his eyes open wide. Joan took in his shock and shook her head at herself, embarrassed that

27

even for a split second she had thought she understood this boy and through him, her son; that she had relied on a tactic that she had to admit had never resulted in any kind of observable success before. Helpless, she watched him look around to find someone to get him out of this. She was about to say, "Never mind, I'm sorry," when she heard him yell in a forceful voice, "Hey, move away, OK? This lady's hurt."

Joan surged with relief for the first time since the pain began and right after, she filled with clean clear surprise: she had gotten it right.

"What's your name?" Joan asked.

"Brandon."

Brandon. Joan had figured he would be "Will" or "Mac" or "Jake" or "Chris", something strong and sure, something she should have named her own son. She thought about all the women her age who attached their newborn babies with these pretentious names and then watched them grow up not being able to fit into them.

"Brandon? I think if you take my hands, I could sit; and then, if you pull me a bit, I could probably get up."

"Yeah, good," Brandon said, with obvious relief. He bent over to reach for her.

Joan took his hands, which were warm and wet with nervous sweat. He had longish blonde hair that fell into his eyes and Joan had a motherly urge to move his bangs, but then he released one hand and moved her hair over her forehead and behind her ear. Without warning or reason, the protective urge inexplicably transformed into an odd uncomfortable romantic one. His gesture was so small but sweet and pure, and his fingers were touching her face. For a second, he left his hand on her cheek, a touch—so tender and so promising all at once—she could not remember ever having felt it before. This was a beautiful boy. No one this beautiful had ever been this close to her before; no one this beautiful had ever touched her face.

"Your hair is in your eyes, Brandon," Joan said, now trying to resist a feeling she didn't know how to embrace and retrieve one she was too used to.

"That's ok, maam," he said, "I can still see you."

"Joan."

"What?"

"My name is Joan," she said because while she fundamentally understood the movie filming in her head would have a tragic ending, at that moment she was so tired of being mom and maam.

"My name is Joan…my friends call me Jo," she said, louder, even though it wasn't true: no one in her life had ever shortened her short name to Jo.

"Come on, Jo," Brandon said, "easy now: sit up."

Fastened tightly to Brandon's hands, Joan moved her head up from the cooler; then as he pulled her toward him, she concentrated on lifting her shoulders but they would not move. She took a breath and tried again to will herself toward Brandon, to move into the strength of his hands but she was frozen to the spot, heavy and solid as a building.

"I can't seem to sit up," she said.

"Sure you can," Brandon replied, with energy this time and he was smiling. "Come on Jo… you can do this."

There was something sure about his voice, his confidence, so Joan held more tightly to his hands and focused her energy on her neck, her head. Lift, she said to herself, damn it: lift.

"I can't move," she said, though she thought that statement was in her head only.

"You can," Brandon said and he moved his hands from her hands up to the part of her arms just below the elbow. His head was bent close; he had green-gray eyes, beautiful skin. Joan could smell him—a little sweat, soap, shampoo. He squatted to get into a better position to lift her and their cheeks were practically touching. Joan gripped his forearms, felt a bubbly surge in her abdomen—the kind that happens to adolescents when they fall in love. What would it be like to kiss a boy like this? she wondered and then shut her eyes in shame, opening them immediately to wonder if there were any girls thinking the same exact thing about her own son. Her heart trembled for all this feeling that was in store for Richie and returned her to herself, replaced the resurrection of her girlhood with the way she wanted to protect her son, the feelings she knew best.

"Brandon," she said quietly, "I am grateful. When you help me up, I'll pay for my groceries and then maybe you can walk me to my car?" She said this like a question, as if she was not sure he would. He nodded. "And then I have something for you," she said, thinking she would give him the wine.

"I'll drive you home, Jo" he said, "and you can make me some tea. Let's just try to get you up now."

Joan held tight to Brandon's forearms. She pushed all of her strength into his strength. She sucked in all the air her lungs would take and braced herself for the pain she knew would accompany lifting her torso from the floor. She imagined herself rising up to him, chest first and then standing. When she got up, she could use the cart to steady herself and Brandon would help her get out of the store.

"Someone better call 911" she heard a voice in the crowd say.

"Already did" someone else replied and Joan was about to say that an ambulance was not necessary: she was just about to stand up. But as she tried to move toward Brandon's pulling, she realized the futility of any attempt: Joan could not get up. Brandon knew it too and very gently, he let her slide back down to the floor.

It took the ambulance about 10 minutes to arrive; during the wait, Brandon sat on the floor and stroked Joan's wet hair. He asked her if she wanted water or a blanket and she said no to both. She was neither thirsty nor cold. And then Brandon reached into his cart and pulled out the package of grapes. He ate two and then fed Joan two: they were still cool, very sweet, and had no seeds. Richie would probably like some grapes, Joan thought. Brandon had maneuvered Joan's head into the crook of his knee.

"So you have a teenage son?" Brandon asked. He had remembered her excuse for being in the snack aisle.

"Yes, a little younger than you, I think."

"I think he should thank me for rescuing his mom," Brandon said.

"I want to thank you, too, Brandon. Look in my cart: I have some excellent wine. I'd like you to have it: you can drink it with your salmon dinner."

"I have an excellent opener; let's drink it together. Now." Brandon pulled the Merlot from her cart and a Swiss Army knife from his pocket. He opened the wine with ease and very carefully set the bottle to her mouth. The wine was delicious; despite Brandon's care, some of it dripped onto her neck and her blouse.

"Sorry," he said.

"Old shirt," Joan replied, and took another sip. "Your turn," she said, and Brandon took a long, appreciative swig.

When the paramedics arrived, they lifted Joan onto the stretcher with tremendous efficiency and minimal pain. Then they began to wheel her toward the door.

"I'm coming," she heard Brandon say.

"Are you her family? Her son?"

"No," Brandon said, still following behind them as if he was.

"Not necessary then, sir."

"No, I'm coming; she needs someone to be with her," he said, and followed them out to the ambulance, the open bottle of Merlot still in his hand. When the paramedics had gotten Joan securely inside, Brandon climbed in. He sat down beside Joan and poured another sip of the wine into her mouth.

"Son?" the paramedic said, "you can't have an open container of alcohol in an ambulance."

But they did because the ambulance was already out of

the Wild Oates parking lot and was turning onto 10th Street. Joan had no idea what was wrong with her, how serious her condition mihgt be, whether her life would change. But she knew Brandon would remain the same, confident, lucky, blessed. She watched him pass the open bottle of merlot under the paramedic's nose and nod his head before he tilted the bottle to Joan's mouth, his other hand cupped under her chin. The paramedic decided just to look away.

Everyone has secrets, Joan thought; some came only so that they could keep themselves.

Lily Brown

The magnificent cause of being,
The imagination, the one reality
In this imagined world

Wallace Stevens, Another Weeping Woman

If you don't start talking immediately after the first hello, a lot of them figure it out and hang up before you have a chance to make the offer. That's one of the problems with this kind of work: there are so many of us out there that people have given up trying to discriminate and just lump us all together as one big pain in the ass.

That's why I am so quick now. As soon as I hear the phone pick up and am sure it's a real voice and not a recorder, I suck in my breath: mid-way through their hello, I am ready to begin.

"Ms. Watkins?" I say Ms. to all women because I don't want to make unmarried women feel bad.

"Yes?"

"Ms. Watkins," (it is good to repeat the name), Hi! (I say HI brightly, especially if I am calling in the morning). My name is Lily Brown and I'm calling to introduce you to a breakthrough in lawn care."

Lily Brown is not my real name, of course, but it sounds real and not threatening. You can't tell my race or religion from it, you can't tell my age. You can't afford to put anyone off in this business.

Sometimes prospective clients hang up right away and when that happens, I just make a note and plan to call back in a couple of days, at a different time of day, and with a different name: Barb Keller, JoAnne Bloom, Cindi Osborne. But other times, a lot of times, when they say, "I'm not interested" I immediately say, "this gardening service gives you a week of pruning and mowing and even some planting for free—as a trial offer."

"Free?" Ah, that's the hook.

That, and knowing exactly what each person I am calling needs.

My success rate is off the charts now, but it wasn't always like this. The reason I am so good at my job now is because I have had a lot of experience; I have learned a lot of lessons.

At my old job, the first one, people used to hang up on me all the time. No matter how sweet or patient or informed I was, some people were just plain rude. My boss told me I had to be polite under all circumstances, but you know that can be very hard when people—total strangers—are mean to you.

Like one time, I called the first person on my list: Alexandra Allen. Nice name, and when she answered I said, "Ms. Alexandra Allen?" (I said it very lyrically) and she said "Yes?" and I said, "Hello! My name is Debbie Rogers and I am calling on behalf of **RingFree Long Distance Service**. Good Morning!" and she said, "I have long distance service, thank you anyway" and I said, "But wait: did you know that **RingFree** offers ten hours of free long distance service..."and she interrupted me and said, "as long as I do what? Sell you my first child?" and she hung up.

That stung. So I called her back about fifteen minutes later and when she answered, I said, "Ms. Allen? It's Debbie from **RingFree** again; listen, I just thought you might want to know that our company wants nothing from you but to give you ten hours of free long distance, ok?" and she said, "Leave me the hell alone" and hung up again. Unfortunately, that call was being recorded by our parent company and that was when the boss said I was not allowed to call back people who declined our offers. Be polite always, he said. He called it my first warning.

I got a second warning about three hours later. It was my thirtieth call or something like that (we try to do ten an hour and then take a break) and I hadn't connected one single person up to **RingFree**. This guy's name was Jack Muldoon and that sounded like a pretty festive name. I was getting tired, which happens to me a lot, and thought I'd try something new.

"Hey Jack-O," I said when he answered, very upbeat and friendly-like, "getting tired of those high priced long distance bills?"

"Who is this?" he said, surprised, and I grabbed the ball: a live one.

"It's me, Jack-O, Maggie Kildare, calling from **RingFree**."

"Who?"

"Maggie. Maggie Kildare, from **RingFree Long Distance Service**, and do I have a deal for you."

"Is this a telemarketer thing?" he wanted to know.

"Not just any telemarketer thing," I said, "in fact, Jackie my boy..."

But he cut me off.

"Look, you freak, I'm not interested: leave me alone" and he slammed down the phone.

I am not a freak.

I hit Redial and when he picked up I said, "Your loss, asshole."

That call was not being monitored but the girl who sat next to me, KiKi Ramirez, reported me to the boss: I got my second warning. I suppose I should have gotten fired for that but it's hard to fire someone like me: I make people uncomfortable. And I have the law on my side.

In the end, I quit that job on my own because their products just would not sell. It was my first telemarketing job but I wasn't discouraged; I figured I had learned a few things there and decided to apply them somewhere else. A couple of weeks later I got a job soliciting magazine subscriptions. Boy, did we offer a lot of magazines, everything you could think of. And we had more freedom at this place—we could ad lib, which I like.

"Ms. Billstein? **StaySlim Magazine** was made just for you!" That was my hook, at first. It worked, too, because women want to stay slim and most of us like things that have been made just for us. I sold three subscriptions to that magazine in my first morning on the job and I was feeling hot.

"Mr. Cochran? Hey, man, do you subscribe to **Car World?**"

"No," Mr. Cochran said, and he sounded intrigued because he drew that No out real long.

"Well, you ought to," I said, "and especially now because it's on sale, if you buy it from me."

"And who might you be?"

"Oh? Didn't I introduce myself? I'm Lydia Shelborne and..."

"Lydia?" he said. "That's a nice name. Where are you calling from?"

"Here at the offices of **Magazines To Go** and we have a very special offer on **Car World** but it expires tomorrow." I was on a roll.

"Really?" he said. Mr. Cochran was definitely interested. And we had this contest going where if you could sell fifteen subscriptions in one day, you'd be eligible for a trip to Mexico. I'm not really one for hanging out at the beach but I thought I might give it to my cousin Alma, who I live with: taking care of me is pretty hard work and Alma could seriously use a vacation.

"So, Mr. Cochran, how would you like to try it for six months? You get the first issue for free!"

"Why don't you call me Harry?" he suggested.

"Sure, Harry, " I agreed. Why not? "So what do you say? If you buy it right now, you'll only pay $1.99 per issue; that's a $2.00 savings off the rack price and you still get Issue No. 1 free."

"Well, I just might, Lydia," he said, "tell me more about it."

I loved this guy. Even though I'd sold three issues of **StaySlim**, I'd also had many hang-ups and a couple of people who kept me on the line too long, thinking the price would go down, and then said no.

"Harry, you'll love this mag. It's big, it's current; it rates cars and publishes articles by race car drivers, mechanics, even celebrities: in the first FREE issue, there's an interview with the CEO of Toyota. It's a great read, Harry, very hot."

"Are you hot, Lydia?" he said, sort of quietly but I heard him. And I was quick to respond, too.

"Oh, I'm hot to give you this great deal, Harry" I said, repeating his name for emphasis.

"What else are you hot to give me, baby? Your pussy?"

"Pervert," I said and hung up the phone. Ruby Schuler, my boss, heard me and came clomping over to my booth. Even though she was obviously over fifty and had what my mother used to call "midrift bulge," she wore danskins as tops and short wrap-around skirts and very high high-heels which she wobbled around in all day. We were cooped up in this warehouse-like room and no one ever saw us so I don't know who she was dressing it up for, but the next day I was back at my cousin Alma's kitchen table looking through the paper for Telemarketer Job #3. That was the first time I was fired but I knew why: no more women bosses for me. I think I threatened old Ruby Schuler. You could see all the gray in her roots and it was embarrassing the way she stood so close to the two guys who worked with us, nudging her hip into one or the other's shoulder while they scanned their phone lists; they didn't even move their eyes from the computer screens when she asked them questions. I also think she didn't like the fact that they would bring me coffee or water or glazed doughnuts without my ever asking, or how on Friday afternoons they would ask me if I needed a ride home or wanted to go out for a drink. I understood what they were doing because I understand a lot of things; I think people mean well but when they ask a person like me if I want to go out and have a drink, they are really trying to see themselves as good people who don't care what strangers in the world think of them. The whole time they imagined what it would be like to show up in a bar with me, they never once thought of what it would be like for me to show up in a bar. I wanted to tell them what I knew and at the same time, I wanted them to thank me for the fact that I always said no. But all I ever said was no and even though I declined weekly invitations from these small, practically hairless men who smelled a little moldy, Ruby hated me because they asked. Some women can be funny that way: every other woman is a threat—even me—no matter how unappealing the prize. Harry the Pervert was a perfect excuse for her to get rid of the competition.

You might think that getting fired for a stupid reason that wasn't even my fault would discourage me from this line of work, but I know telemarketing is my calling. Hey, no pun intended. I know this is the kind of work I was meant to do: I can feel it in my bones, which are a little soft and ache sometimes but they tell me what I need to know.

"You have a pleasant voice," the guy from the ad I called said to me over the phone. "Why don't you come on in?"

"I have experience, too," I chimed, trying to show off my voice.

As soon as I got out of the van, I knew this job wasn't for me: first, the office was on the eighth floor with only a service elevator. I took it up there for the interview but it gave me the creeps. I'm not in a position to discriminate about elevators but this one looked like a cage, creaked through every inch of its pulley, and had two of its three bulbs burnt out. On the way up, I already knew I was going to have to ask the guy to have the elevator inspected.

When I finally landed and rolled into the office, there was only the guy I talked to on the phone and one other guy working there. They were selling exercise equipment but the room was full of cigarette smoke and these two guys didn't look too fit. Apparently, I wasn't what they were looking for either. Before they asked me a single interview question, the guy I talked to on the phone said, "I don't think this is going to work, Miss...uh, Miss?" I hadn't given them my name yet.

"Atlas," I said, "Jonnie May Atlas" because I thought

maybe they would get the connection and regret not hiring me (even though I didn't want the job) and then I wheeled around and said, "I don't think so, either. See ya" and back I went into the horror-movie elevator; I held my breath until it creaked down to the first floor.

My cousin Alma said I could probably get a job at **Food World** where she worked, maybe back in the office checking orders and calling them in, although I didn't think that would be enough for me. I need a challenge. I need to negotiate. I need to make deals. But after going on a bunch more interviews and not being able to find a telemarketing job (Alma thought maybe the word had gotten around about me, but I didn't see how that could happen: Miami is a huge city and, after all, I'd only had two jobs), I decided to take Alma up on her offer. I figured that maybe if I was calling in orders from the back office, I could strike up some good phone relationships with vendors or customers with delinquent bills, practice my negotiating skills and in a while, go back on the telemarketing job search.

The grocery store where Alma worked was small and dusty; actually, it was more like a market. It was owned by these two brothers who weren't American but I didn't know what they were and never really cared to ask. They took turns at the cash register and all the while, smoked cigarettes and drank some rank orange drink out of chipped coffee mugs while Alma stocked shelves or put old sliced cold cuts under a slice or two of fresh ones in the deli case. When she wasn't busy, she tried to dust the tops of canned soups, fruit and vegetables but some of that stuff had been there for so long that the dust had turned to permanently attached grime. The brothers liked Alma, though, and I think they felt sorry for me since I was having a hard time getting a job, so they said Sure, she can work here and there I was.

When she brought me in, they looked at me and then said I could try being the cashier. I was surprised but Alma freaked out: she said, "In the store? With customers?" The brothers looked at her funny but I understood: I'm not exactly Cindy Crawford.

And, in fact, I didn't think it was a good idea either to have me face to face with people buying food. But the brothers said that if I did cash register duty all day long, it would free them up to pay more attention to what went on in the store. After I'd been there a couple of days, I knew nothing went on in the store but you know what? If it hadn't been for that job, I wouldn't be where I am today.

They put me behind the cash register counter, where they also sold gum and candy, batteries, TV Guide, refrigerator magnets, postcards that said "Welcome to Miami" and condoms. Many kinds of condoms. And one good thing was that I was not a threat to people buying condoms. I had a high chair that raised me above the counter and my fingers, which were already nimble from dialing phone numbers so efficiently, were good at ringing up purchases.

The brothers stayed by the front door all the time now, drinking their nasty orange drinks and smoking these unfiltered cigarettes and nodding to customers when they came in. They were sinister looking but people in the neighborhood seemed to be used to them. At least the store was pretty busy.

I, on the other hand, apparently took some time to get used to. People would walk in, see me, and stop in their tracks. A couple of people actually gasped. People are afraid of change, I guess, but I am the master of change, so I was pretty understanding. Still, the brothers would have none of it. "These crazy peoples," they said, "what do they know?"

One day, one of the brothers—he called himself Butch but I knew that wasn't his real name—told this customer that Alma and I were sisters. I figured out that he was trying to get these people to like me—the new girl—so he made up this lie: turns out, this brother was smarter than I thought because this phony news was a big hit. This older woman customer, with her hair in what my mother used to call a "babushka," smiled and said, "How nice: two sisters and two brothers" and she lingered at the deli and bought two different kinds of sliced cheese from

Alma. Butch must've like that because he and his brother, who went by the fake name of Lou, started telling everyone that me and Alma were sisters, two sisters who worked for two brothers. Pretty soon, when customers came to me to buy their old meat and wrapped cheese and Brillo pads, they'd say things like, "you look just like your sister" or "how nice you work with your sister. She looks after you," thinking I was younger I guess, which I am, but still. I don't look anything like Alma: she's tall and skinny and has red hair.

I stayed at the store for about eight weeks and I was starting to get pretty bored because all you get to say is "$12.42 please. Thank you." But then something happened that gave me a brainstorm plan. All along, people would just start talking about stuff while I rang up their groceries. But this one day, a middle-aged woman said, "do you know of a good dry cleaner around here? My car broke down and I have to walk everywhere now." I didn't know about dry cleaners in the neighborhood because I didn't drive or walk and also because I had a limited amount of clothes that Alma washed and that I just wore over and over again. But I felt bad about not being able to give out good information; after all, by then I knew that offering deals was what I was born to do. The next day, a guy who looked like a college student came in; he was carrying an armful of books and when he came up to the register for me to ring up his liter of Coke and two bags of Sour Cream and Salsa Doritos, he said, "Think these'll get me through this paper I have to write? And then type?" Later that same day, another woman—a young one with two little kids pulling at her pants and relentlessly asking for gum—said, "Can I leave them here with you for awhile?" She was kidding but apparently the kids didn't realize that because they were staring at me and screaming "No!" and promising to be good, but it gave me an idea.

"Hey, Butch," I said later the same day, "you know what we need?"

"Huh?" he said. I suspected there was something in that

orange drink clearly impairing his verbal skills.

"We need a bulletin board, for people who need things. You know, like babysitting or rides somewhere or typing? This is a neighborhood store: people could use that kind of thing."

Butch didn't answer me. However, the next day, there was a bulletin board nailed up beside the counter.

"Tell people," Butch said and Lou nodded in agreement. Men of few words.

"Sure," I said, "I'll just do that." This was my project. I told all my customers that we now had a bulletin board where people could request goods and services. Or offer them, if they had any.

At first, the bulletin board business was slow. Nothing happened at all for the first few days and although I was used to waiting for the big pay-off from my weeks as a telemarketer, the truth is I was getting impatient. But then I got another idea. I put up some requests under pseudonyms: "Blind girl needs to be read to twice a day. Good money: please call 305-622-9485" and I used the name Miranda DeLauer. Next to that I had a Frank Riccolini asking for someone to shop for his aged mother, three times a week. I felt really pleased about these two ads, partly because it reminded me of how good I was at making up names. I placed a small pad of paper and a pencil next to the bulletin board and pointed out the requests when people came in.

I am a lot smarter than people think when they see me. Three young guys came in for beer and were about ninety cents short; I gave it to them, anyway, but then suggested they write down Miranda and Frank's numbers so they could earn some money and pay for their beer. Then Mrs. Ruiz from down the street put her own ad up, requesting someone to clean her house. She made a sign with the pencil stating her name and her need and then her number in a row of tear-off sheets at the bottom. I tore two off, just to make it competitive.

A day or so later, the young guys came back in, separately, saying that no one answered at those numbers they called;

Frank Riccolini, one guy said, didn't even exist. I tried to be casual about that, and then immediately suggested that if they were looking for work, why didn't they put their skills and talents up on the board and see who called.

By the end of three weeks, the bulletin board was thriving. The guys got a lot of work and even bought me a present to thank me for helping them. It's a pair of terrycloth wrist-bands and it makes resting my arms on the high chair much more comfortable. And so many people needed so many things that Butch and Lou had to get a bigger board.

When I saw that oversized bulletin board filled with needs and offers and people stopping to look at it when they came in and out of the store, I knew that my work there at **Food World** was done. At the same time, I had a brilliant idea (which, obviously, is my strong point). But I am not an impulsive girl; I couldn't quit Butch and Lou until I had my next project all set up. So everyday for the next week or so, while I was waiting by the door for Alma to wipe down the last counter and punch out, I pulled off a few numbers from the board. After I'd gotten about a dozen numbers of people who needed things, I told Alma the work was too much for me.

"You tired?" she asked. She was tired all the time so she understood.

"All the time," I said, and yawned for effect. I hated to trick Alma who was so good to me and cared for me a lot but I knew in the end that what I was planning would pay off big for both of us.

"All right, darlin'," she replied, "I'll tell the boys you need some time off. You can stay home and watch the programs, tell me who's screwing who." Before Alma got her job at the market, we used to watch all the daytime soaps together. We had a little money from the State so we didn't have to worry so much about working. But then we had needs, mostly me, so Alma got this job and I watched the programs until it was clear that TV was just too passive a pastime for me.

"We'll be all right for a while, sweetie," she said. "You need to rest."

That's how I got to where I am now, but this time it's much easier, I'm much more successful, and I don't have some boss breathing down my neck all the time. Besides, I know what people need now so I just use that knowledge and my skills and call them up. In the last two weeks, I've only had one person say no and that's because she'd ended up typing the paper herself. But everybody else I call says yes. My clients are nice, cheery, and polite. And they are grateful.

Mrs. B., I guess she didn't want to use her full name, was so happy when I called to say I was Bernadette Kelleher from **BabyBeGood**, a new child care center in the neighborhood. Mrs. B. is a serious Catholic; she used to come into the store every Sunday after Church and buy two pounds of honey ham to make sandwiches for her kids' lunch. I knew if I had the name of a saint, she'd trust me immediately. And she did.

Then I called "Roy," the guy with only one arm. He needed help around the house and when he answered the phone I said, "Mr. Roy? This is your lucky day: **Helping Hands Inc.** has a special offer for you."

"**Helping Hand?**" he said, "what is that?"

"We do odd jobs, Mr. Roy: shopping, cooking, painting, plumbing (I knew his toilet had been on the fritz because he bought a plunger: Butch and Lou had all kinds of weird stuff in their store), cleaning. Whatever you need. And if you sign up with us now, we'll give you our first two services for half price."

Mr. Roy thanked me six times before I hung up the phone.

I had a little more work to do with Ms. Watkins and the lawn care job but eventually she came around; her crew, I told her, would show up Saturday morning around 9:00. They were a husband and wife team, I explained (she's single and nervous and I knew she'd feel better if there was a wife around), and their specialty was fruit trees. One time, Ms. Watkins, whose first name is Louise, bought some small shriveled oranges at the market and told me that soon, when her own oranges ripened, she'd only be coming into the store for toilet paper and laundry soap.

I have found the secret: figure out exactly what people really need and then call up and offer it to them. New long distance service, magazines, more credit cards, butt-busters...those are things people don't really want and certainly don't need and never even think about until some faceless stranger breaks into the phone lines and tells them they can't live without these things in a message from a pre-printed card. It's hard to believe in a voice that can't even pronounce your name correctly. I never have that problem now. And although in some way I am faceless when I call, in a more important way I'm not: I have seen all of my clients. And they have seen me, even though they don't know it's me when I call with offers. But deep down we know each other: I know what each one needs. When you can call up a real person and know they need clothes washed or lawns mowed or dogs walked, then you are in business: you are not just some do-gooder trying to make yourself feel better and you are not just some capitalist trying to make money off unsuspecting consumers and you are not just some pathetic drone calling strangers all day so you can make enough money to go out and drink beer and get smashed and then get in your car at two o'clock in the morning and plow into the back of a Dogde Dart carrying a tired family of three home from a vacation, sending the sleeping thirteen year old over the front seat and face first through the windshield. No: you are a good person spending your valuable time in a genuine effort to give people what they need.

In our neighborhood, there's a range of needs and I am a range of good girls with nice names to fill them. Since I left **Food World**, I've been Annie Cox, babysitter; Suzanne Bolton, driver of widows to doctors and dentists and podiatrists; Carrie Bodine, grocery shopper and errand runner; Elizabeth Brown, reader for the blind; Alexis Crane, girl mechanic; EllaMae Warden, house-cleaner; and I've been a manicurist, lawn care professional, pastry-maker, yoga instructor, housepainter and pet groomer.

And I manage to watch the stories for Alma, too.

Speaking of Alma, lately she's begun to fret about our money situation, mostly because I'm not bringing any in. That's the only part of this business I haven't figured out yet. Now that I've got all the clients and their trust—now that I've finally figured out how to convince people that I have what they need—I need to find the people to do the jobs. My approach may seem ass-backward but, as usual, I have a plan. I'm going to tell Alma I want to go back and cashier for a while at **Food World**. I'll tell her I'm bored at home, that all this rest has made me restless. Alma will be pleased because I think she liked having me with her: she could watch me and make sure I ate and took my medicine; she could put cream on my face and arms three times a day. She liked being able to rub my legs at noon and again around three. She might be a little sorry that I won't be keeping up with the stories, but you know what? I bet Butch and Lou would probably buy me one of those little TVs: they don't really like running the cash register and besides, around 2:00 in the afternoon, they're about ready to say yes to anything.

And it won't be so bad; I have my wrist-bands and to tell you the truth, I miss some of the customers. The homeless guy who lives in the store doorway after we close used to pet my knee when I got to work; I couldn't feel it but I saw the gesture and it means something when someone is not afraid to touch you. And I miss the girls who work in the restaurant across the street; they used to come in on Friday afternoons for beer and chips and the cheap condoms; they called me Lily and always said, "You never know, Lily: this could be the weekend...". And I'm thinking if I could talk to more customers, ask them what they do in their spare time, if they have anything to offer, I could eventually have two boards—one with requests and one with solutions: then I could set everyone up. Balance, that's what I like: knowing who needs what out there and knowing who can provide. When I have enough matches, I'll get tired again. It might hurt business at **Food World** when I leave but if things go the way I think they will, I'll be back. Or maybe Alma and I will have so much more money, we can retire. Or at least go to Disney World. Maybe Butch and Lou would want to come; they keep saying they need a vacation and I've heard them mention "that mouse in Orlando."

Who knows? One thing I've learned from the fact that I stayed in this world is that everybody needs something. And everybody needs someone, maybe even someone like me, someone with a lot of time and patience, some brains and some experience helping the truly helpless get what they really need.

Dani

Slivers of rain upon the pane.
Jade-green with sunlight, melt and flow
Upward again—they leave no stain
Of all the storm an hour ago.

Hart Crane, Echoes

On Thursday afternoon, a woman walked into The Crystal Market holding a huge unwrapped head of red leaf lettuce. Her right hand was bandaged. She was so angry, she was shaking.

"Look at *this*," she said to Brian, the produce manager, and pried back some lettuce leaves to reveal scattered carpenter's nails. Earlier, at home, she had grabbed the lettuce to wash it and a nail went through the soft skin between her middle and ring fingers.

"How did this happen?" she demanded.

Brian could not answer.

"What are you going to do about it? I'm going to sue you and this store." She stood there waiting for Brian to respond, but he did not: he had no idea what those nails were doing in that lettuce or what he could do about it.

"How could this have happened, Brian? What if I hadn't seen these and fed this lettuce to my children?" She was waving her hands, causing nails to fall from the lettuce she held, and she was tapping her foot rapidly on the floor.

"Mrs. Hill, I'm sorry. I don't know what happened, how this happened. But I'm definitely going to find out. Here, how about this: you shop for free next week, ok? Whatever you want, no matter how much. Come every day. And I'll pick your produce out for you myself."

Mrs. Hill's hands dropped to her sides and the lettuce fell to the floor. She stood still for a few seconds staring at Brian as if she thought he could produce an explanation; then, without a word, she turned and walked toward the General Manager's office.

Brian picked up the lettuce and examined it. Then he went to the lettuce section and looked around; could a light panel have fallen, dropping nails? Wouldn't he have seen that? Wondering about the other heads of unwrapped lettuce, he started lifting random leaves from various heads but all he saw was what he expected to see, the paler bottoms of the soft leaves, little nubs of dark soil. Maybe it happened at the suppliers? He would call them immediately.

On his way to his own office, he saw his boss, Will Hogan, coming across the main aisle. Brian waited.

"How are you doing, buddy?" Will asked. He put his hand on Brian's shoulder.

"I don't know, Will. I don't know how to explain it."

"Well, Mrs. Hill took you up on your offer: mighty generous."

"Sorry, Will, but it was the first thing that came out of my mouth."

"No problem: she's been shopping here a long time; besides, she might have decided never to come back here again if you hadn't come up with that offer. But we're going to have to figure out what happened. You ok, though?"

Will knew how seriously Brian took his job at The Crystal Market. It was an unusual thing to see a guy like Brian—handsome, polished, well-educated—so devoted to a job buying and stocking and taking care of produce. When he first hired Brian, he thought the boy—then around twenty-two years old—would last the summer and then take off to find a more lucrative and professional position. But now, five years later, Brian considered the fruit and vegetable department his own: customers knew and loved him; suppliers respected his seriousness and earnestness and were careful never to stiff him with rotting fruit on the bottoms of the crates; mothers left their children with him to help stack peppers or apples while they went off to finish their shopping.

"I'm still in 'Marketing', I guess," Brian had joked the one day that Will asked him if he planned on doing anything with his business degree from the University of Miami. After that, Will resolved that the boy would stay as long as he would stay and it was turning out to be for the long haul.

"Don't take this personally, son; it's a freak thing. Could've happened to anybody," Will assured him, though he looked as though he was not so sure he believed it himself.

"Yeah, I guess," Brian said, despondently, "but I just don't see how. I receive everything myself. I'm checking the stock continually. Usually, I'm even picking out the produce for customers myself."

"Well, let's not panic. Take a look through and see if you can figure out what happened. Call Marcelli's and see if they've had any shipment problems. If we don't find anything, we'll just have to assume that one head of lettuce was in the wrong place at the wrong time. Just be glad no one got hurt."

Brian spent the day examining as much of his stock as he could; he called Marcelli's but they were as shocked as he was. He talked to a few of the people who worked for him in Produce but no one could figure out how all of those tiny nails ended up in Mrs. Hill's lettuce. Briefly, he wondered if maybe she had put them there herself, but that seemed absurd: she had been shopping at The Crystal Market long before Brian got there and she was, like many of the customers, a sweet and down-to-earth person. Although the day passed without incident, the mystery did not weaken for Brian: he was nervous and suspicious, eyeing customers he'd known for five years, following people he didn't recognize down the aisles. He did not sleep well and was back at work very early the next morning.

When Dani came into the store, she saw Brian touching the parsnips and turnips, rolling them around; he was wearing rubber gloves.

"Taking your love affair with this job a little too far, aren't you?" she asked, lifting a cellophane package of celery.

"Wait," Brian said urgently, "let me see that." He felt around the stalks and flicked through the leaves exposed at the open top; satisfied that the celery was safe, he set it gently into Dani's cart. He didn't want to scare her by telling her about the nails in Mrs. Hill's leaf lettuce but he wasn't taking any chances either.

"What's up with you? You look like you're about to perform a vegetablecotmy."

"Yeah," Brian said. Although he was still unnerved by Mrs. Hill's nails, he was always unnerved by Dani. For the last year, she had come into the store like clockwork every Tuesday and Friday at 9:00 am, yet even though he knew she was coming, her appearance always made him skip a breath. She was so beautiful, with jade green eyes and short very black curly hair. She wore tiny bright blue sapphire earrings and the palest pink lipstick. No matter what he was doing, when Dani came into the store Brian stayed with her as long as she was in his department.

Brian and Dani had developed a friendship based on produce. She was as particular about what she bought as he was about what he stocked. In the process of discussing the virtues of organic growing, apples from Washington versus apples from Pennsylvania, which onions were truly sweeter—Walla Walla or Vidalia—they'd gotten to know a little bit about each other, too. Dani told him she was an art therapist; she had just moved to Miami right before they met but in the entire year, she had not been able to find a job. The positions were few and far between for Dani; because she had just finished her Master's degree and only had some internship experience, she was often a potential employer's third or fourth choice.

One morning about five months ago, after picking out peppers and eggplants and zucchinis for Dani—she was going home to make ratatouille and told Brian she would bring him some later in the week—Brian asked her if she'd like to have breakfast. He had just finished stocking for the morning and was hungry; Will often let him take an hour or so to go to Berries, the health food café next door.

Over cranberry-almond granola and tea, Dani explained art therapy. Troubled children, mostly from the inner city, often had difficulty talking about their problems: either they were reluctant to talk or they simply did not possess the language skills to communicate. What Dani did was have them draw or paint or work with clay when language was not available to them; somehow, this form of expression opened avenues to the kind of communicating these kids needed to do.

Dani was an artist, too: she painted and made three-dimensional collages. She asked Brian if he had ever taken any art courses because his vegetable displays were so original, so beautiful.

At first, he just started laughing at the idea that he was artistic since his whole educational career had focused on math and business. But then he confessed that sometimes at night, he fell asleep imagining how he might arrange a shipment of multi-colored peppers or grapes; he'd come to work very early the next morning and he described to Dani the process by which his vegetable displays would begin to take the shape of the visions he had for them. Sometimes, he said, when he was finished, he would feel a kind of peace that nothing else brought and he was able to carry that contentment with him all day, no matter what else happened that threatened to disrupt it.

Dani had been listening to him so intently that he just kept talking; somehow, he got around to telling her how sometimes when he had little kids helping him create the vegetable displays, they would start saying private things. He had never told anyone, not even Will, some of the things these kids had said.

"One time a kid, maybe he was seven, was helping me put these giant strawberries in a row. I said they looked like hearts and then he stopped stacking. I asked him why he stopped and he said, 'if they're like hearts, I might crush them.' And I said, 'no you won't' and he said 'yeah, I will, because I crush Mommy's heart all the time.'"

"What did you do?" Dani had asked, pushing her bowl away and leaning over the table, her chin cupped in her hand.

"I said something really stupid like, 'hey, Benjy, don't worry about that: you're doing a great job.' Something stupid like that."

"That wasn't stupid, Brian, it was good. Did he start working again?"

"Yeah, he did."

"See?" Dani said, smiling. She had perfect teeth.

There were a few other breakfasts after that; each time, they got to know each other better. Dani loved to grow things, but in Miami she didn't have a yard. So she had planted an urban garden; in little pots on her small back porch, she grew herbs and cherry tomatoes and chili peppers. Dani's sister, who she had come to Miami to live with, had a high-powered job in the Mayor's office; she went to work early and came home late. Since Dani wasn't bringing in any money, she felt the least she could do was shop and then cook dinner for her sister. From her descriptions of the dishes she invented, Brian knew Dani must be a great cook. Brian was just beginning to learn how to cook, something he had never thought much about until Will had put him in charge of produce. Over the early months of their friendship, Dani had given Brian some recipes. And they had some other things in common, too.

"I can't believe you hated **Titanic**: I thought I was the only person in the world who squirmed and yawned through that endless movie," Dani had said.

"I can't believe I admitted that to you." Brian was nervous around Dani. He wanted to impress her. As soon as he'd said he'd hated **Titanic**, he was sure she would say she loved it and he cringed at what he knew was the great irony in his personality: when he ought to say something to someone, he often clammed up and couldn't speak; when he wanted to be more careful and consider his words before they came out, he blurted out statements he immediately wished he could take back. But when Dani agreed with him about the movie, he felt himself relax; he was so relieved that he leaned over the table as if he was going to kiss her. Luckily, he caught himself, stopped cold, sat back.

While they ate, he watched himself—were his elbows on the table? Did he chew with his mouth open? He tried to be careful about everything—what he said and how he said it, whether his breath was bad, if there was crust in eyes, if his cowlick was up. He couldn't explain it but there was something about this calm and beautiful girl that made Brian completely self-conscious about things he normally paid little attention to. But there was also something so effortless about being with Dani that after they'd said goodbye, he realized he couldn't remember all that he had said or how it had come out. At the end of every meal with Dani, Brian was sorry that he had to go back to work, sorry that he couldn't help her find a job, and more sorry than usual about Maureen.

Right at this moment, he was sorry he couldn't leave to go to breakfast because he still had so much produce to inspect. He had not been able to talk to anyone about the nail incident and he felt sure now Dani would listen and understand his fear. Maybe she would know what to do.

But instead he said, "What else do you need today?" He stepped behind her as she began to move her cart down the aisle.

"I don't know; I have to look around." Dani pushed her cart farther away.

"Any news on the job front?" He watched over her selections.

"Not really," she said, turning a head of broccoli over, "I had a couple of good interviews last week. No calls yet, though. Is that cauliflower fresh?"

"Yeah, but we have brand new ones in the back: let me go get you one."

"Thanks." Dani waited near the broccoli and cauliflower,

displayed like cascading prehistoric flowers under the lights. She fingered the broccoli again and looked over at the peppers. As Brian headed back toward Dani, he saw her looking at the display—red, green, yellow, orange, purple—set up like a rainbow. He wondered if she was impressed, if she thought the arrangement was artistic.

Today Brian was running a special on mixed types of mushrooms—porcini, shitake, portabellas—when he returned with the cauliflower, he suggested Dani buy some. "You could make that risotto you were telling me about."

"Did I mention that?" she said lightly, "that's nice you remembered. Yeah, I'll have a pound of those mixed mushrooms."

"I'll pick them for you." Brian picked carefully. Although he was trying to convince himself that Mrs. Hill's nail infested lettuce was a freak occurrence, he couldn't be too sure.

"Do you use vegetable stock in that?" He placed the mushrooms in her cart, but Dani had her back to him and didn't answer. She had moved on to look at the parsley and cilantro. Maybe she hadn't heard him.

"What kind of liquid do you use in the risotto?" He was still trying to make conversation, to prolong Dani's time in the produce aisle, but still she didn't respond. Obviously, she was preoccupied, no doubt because of her job search, he thought. It was nearly the middle of July and she had been looking for over a year now. He wondered if maybe he could leave for just half an hour, to buy her a cup of tea. Brian watched her scan the tomatoes, turning different ones over and then putting them back: he wanted to do something nice for Dani. He also wanted to talk to her about Mrs. Hill and the nails. As soon as she had gotten all her produce, he resolved, he would see if maybe later in the afternoon, she might have time to get some tea.

By the time they reached the end of the aisle, Brian had selected pears, cooking apples, organic greens from the open bin (this took some time, as Brian was covertly feeling for nails), yellow wax beans, brussel sprouts, carrots and bean sprouts for Dani.

She thanked him, as usual, but then didn't linger as she usually did. Brian panicked.

"Hey," he called after her, just as she turned the corner toward canned goods, "do you want to have breakfast?"

"What?" Dani turned and stopped.

Wasn't he going to ask her to come back later? He tried to double-back.

"Uh, do you want to have breakfast again sometime?" God that sounded stupid.

"Sure. Sometime," she said laughing and turned away.

Throughout the rest of the day, no matter how much work he did or how diligent he was in helping customers, Brian kept hearing Dani. Sure. Sometime. Why couldn't he have just made a plan? Or a real date?

But he knew the reason why he couldn't make a real date: Maureen. Brian and Maureen had been together since high school; they went to University of Miami together and now lived a block away from each other. Maureen was in medical school. Both of their families were just waiting for them to get engaged, though Brian's was also waiting for him to "straighten up" and get a "real job." But like his inability to leave The Crystal Market, he was unable to leave Maureen, even though the reasons were at completely opposite ends of the spectrum: he loved his work at the market.

He hadn't told Maureen about his meals with Dani: there was no reason to, at least until he figured out a way to break up. Maureen had come to college in Miami to be with Brian because he wanted to study international business there; she had decided to stay for medical school because of him, too, even though she wanted to be back in Chicago. Her commitment and sacrifice was not lost on him but it didn't lure him to honesty, either. Beside, he and Dani were just friends who had impromptu bagels or cereal at the café next door. There was nothing to tell. And their meals weren't anything like dates; in fact, because Dani insisted, they always split the bill.

Except for the last time, which was just this past Tuesday. Over apricot waffles and a new kind of green tea, Dani had asked him if he ever thought about opening a market of his own. He had, and he pulled a pen from his shirt pocket and began to draw on a napkin the floor plan for the market he wanted to build. The next thing he knew, as he drew the section that would house only organic fruits and vegetables, he was telling her his whole life story. His father was a big executive at a major Chicago ad firm and had a job waiting for him; he explained how he'd taken this job at the Crystal for the summer after graduating from college but just never left, how that caused problems with his family because they wanted him to come home and get serious. But he was serious, he thought: no, he knew he was serious, a serious person. He just wasn't ready for his father's life. And he wasn't ready to marry Maureen, either.

When he had gotten to this fact of his story, Brian saw that Dani was staring at him with what he took for wonder. She put down her fork and pushed her plate of unfinished waffles away. He was sure she was thinking what he had thought all along: why didn't everyone just leave him alone and let him do what made him happy? So he went on. He described his family—how everyone did what they were supposed to do. His older brother was a lawyer; his younger brother was working on an MBA; the youngest person in his family, his sister Kerrie, had just finished college and was engaged. There was a lot of family pressure for Brian to do what he was supposed to do: get a professional job, make money, get married. And then he told Dani about the palpable pressure from Maureen. As he spoke, he heard himself saying things that he hadn't even realized were true before: all of the pressure just made him more attentive to the produce in the market, and more loyal to Will, who treated him like an equal and like a son—a son who made him proud.

"Will gives me free reign," Brian said, "and he is really happy with what I've done with the department. I do everything in there now: I'm responsible for the whole thing. I know it sounds stupid, but that produce department is the most important thing in my life."

"More important than Maureen?" Dani had asked, in a snide tone of voice he had not heard her use before; she did not look at him and was reaching for her purse.

"Well, yeah...no...I don't know" he had said, flustered then because he knew that Maureen had become the least important thing—even less important than picking out vegetables for Dani—but, as usual, he didn't know how to say it. He started to work on his drawing again.

He had managed to say more to her than he had said to anyone else he knew, and he had finished the layout of his dream market as well. He presented it to her. "Talk about art therapy," he said, embarrassed, "I should pay you for this session."

"No," Dani had said quickly, "in fact, let me pay for this meal," and she laid down the full amount, plus a tip that seemed inordinately generous, especially for someone who wasn't working. Then she claimed to be in a big hurry and left the café before he'd even had a chance to stand up.

Thinking about it now, Brian realized, her departure seemed odd. All along, he thought she liked him in the way he liked her: he caught her staring at him when he looked her way, he felt in ways he couldn't articulate that they communicated in smiles and gestures that didn't exactly need words. But Dani never actually told him anything personal and he realized that he didn't really know her.

Still, he wanted to see her again. The closer he got to Dani, the closer he got to breaking up with Maureen because Dani—with her bright green eyes and smooth skin and the way she focused in on him—made him feel things deep inside that he had never felt for Maureen. But today he had blown it and Dani wouldn't be back in the store until Tuesday. Brian returned to the produce department and began to prepare for the Friday rush.

That night, Brian slept uneasily. He kept waking up and thinking it was time to go to work or, because he was dreaming, thinking it was time to go home from work. At one point in the middle of the night, he woke up in a sweat thinking his alarm hadn't gone off and he had missed a breakfast date with Dani. Just before sinking back into his final hour of sleep, he resolved he would make a definite plan with Dani when she came into the store on Tuesday morning. And he would talk to Maureen.

The next morning, Saturday, while Brian was arranging the new shipment of purple potatoes, using a soft cloth to wipe away bits of soil, he heard his name being called over the PA system.

"Brian, please come to the Manager's Office. Brian— Manager's Office."

Brian set the cloth on the cart with the boxes of fresh potatoes and went to Will's office. Usually when Will needed him, he just came and found him in Produce. Brian wondered what was up.

Two young men were sitting in Will's office; there was a head of broccoli on his desk.

"Brian, this is Mr. Gomez and Mr. Ardagio; they are new customers, new to the neighborhood." Brian said hello and shook each one's hand; he did not recognize them.

"Brian." Will paused and was clearly uncomfortable. "Brian," he began again, "these two gentlemen were in here last night and they bought, among other things, this head of broccoli." Brian looked at the broccoli; it looked fine, if a little worn from sitting on Will's desk for who knew how long. Brian shrugged and smiled, but he was aware of the anxiety swelling in his stomach.

"Look on the bottom," Mr. Ardagio said, "go on: look. Pick it up."

"But be careful," added Mr. Gomez.

Gingerly, Brian picked up the broccoli, examining the flowery head carefully. He saw nothing out of line; but when he turned it over to examine the stalk, he saw a piece of green glass had been wedged inside. The flat bottom of the glass was visible on the stalk's edge.

"Oh, God" was all Brian could think to say.

"Brian," Will said, in his quiet way, "obviously we will be giving Mr. Ardagio and Mr. Gomez as many groceries as they can carry home today, but do you have any idea how this might have happened?"

"No idea. None at all," Brian said, and automatically just slumped into the chair he was standing in front of. "No idea," he repeated, "no idea."

Will sent the two customers out into the store to shop for whatever they wanted, for free, and he also told them to be sure to select pastries from the on-site bakery as well. Then he sat down at his desk and stared at Brian.

"What the hell is going on?"

"I wish I knew," Brian said, and it was true. This was the most bizarre thing that had ever happened to Brian in his whole life and he told Will so.

"What are we going to do," his boss asked.

Brian thought for a minute. "I don't know. I'll go over every piece of fruit and vegetable myself today, again" he said, "and I'll call every supplier. Have there been other complaints?"

"Not a one," Will said, "But this goes beyond complaints, son; someone could get hurt. Imagine swallowing glass. At the least, we could get sued."

Immediately Brian thought of Dani, of the cauliflower he had gone to the back to get for her, and of all the produce she had bought the day before. Did she buy broccoli? He couldn't remember. Dani's sister's favorite dish was Dani's broccoli pesto over spaghetti. He couldn't remember if she'd taken a broccoli or not. And he tried to remember who else had been in yesterday and what they had purchased, but he resolved then and there that he would call Dani as soon as he left Will.

"I know, I know," Brian responded. "I'll keep a closer watch. I'll talk to the other produce people. I'll double, I'll triple check everything. I don't know what else to do."

"Well," Will replied, "let's assume this is a some coincidence, although I'm getting nervous."

"It has to be a coincidence," Brian said, "a freak thing."

"You're right," Will agreed, "who knows what happens between picking and packaging and shipping and delivery? I'll help you keep tabs. Maybe we can hire one or two more people part-time to help you out, move some of the staff around. That way, employees can hand-pick items for customers and without their knowing, troubleshoot."

"Good idea," Brian said, and he was standing now because suddenly the image of Dani laughing with her sister while she ate broccoli pesto flecked with jagged glass went through his mind. "Listen, Will?" he said, "I'm really sorry. You know, this job is my world."

"We'll just have to be more careful."

After asking Ruth and Louise who had been stocking shelves to watch over produce, to help customers, Brian sprinted upstairs to his small office. He picked up the phone to dial before realizing that he didn't know Dani's number. They hadn't exchanged numbers. It wasn't that kind of relationship; but the way Brian felt at that moment—breathless and unable to swallow—he realized that he wanted it to be that kind of relationship. He would tell Maureen about Dani tomorrow night. Even if Dani didn't want him, he would tell Maureen that although he couldn't explain it, he was falling in love with girl who he barely knew.

Brian went to the phone book to look up "Newman"— at least he knew that much. And Dani lived in the neighborhood so he thought he would be able to recognize the street.

"Shit," he said out loud, when he saw the number of D. Newman's in the phone book; he scanned the "D. Newman" list but didn't see a single familiar street name. Well, of course, he thought: she moved here to live with her sister. But he didn't know her sister's first name. He stood up and started pacing his small office, back and forth between the desk and the wall. Who knows what could have been in those mushrooms? The apples? You could hide anything in an apple or a squash and no one would know. Now he imagined Dani's mouth full of mushroom risotto or stewed apples, tiny nails and pieces of broken glass tearing up her throat as she swallowed.

But she would have come in, or the sister would have come in. If it was really terrible, it would have been on the news.

There was a hard knock on his office door and Brian jumped up to get it. Although he knew it wouldn't be Dani, he had a vision that it would be and the disappointment clearly registered on his face when he opened the door.

"Hey, what's with you, man?" It was Luis, the stock boy, who stood there for a second taking in the look on Brian's face. "Listen, there are a ton of customers in produce now. You got to come down."

For the rest of the weekend, no one came in to complain about the produce. Brian and his staff and other store employees tried to hand pick as much produce for customers as they could. Still, there were too many people. Brian wondered about Dani continually, though the image of her bleeding to death from sabotaged produce receded as the hours passed. Of course, she did not come in on the weekend—she never did—but in the back of Brian's mind, he hoped. In fact, he thought he saw her: once he was carrying a crate of bananas out from the store room and when he set it down, he thought he caught a glimpse of the back of a head of short black hair but by the time he ran down the main aisle looking, he saw no one who even remotely resembled her. Then, on Sunday, he looked up from arranging stalks of fresh brussel sprouts in a sunburst pattern because he heard a voice saying "No thank you, I'm fine" and he was sure it was Dani. But when he scanned the area, she wasn't there. You are going crazy, he said to himself, you're hallucinating. She'll be in Tuesday. Relax.

On Sunday evening, Maureen came over for dinner; normally, Brian tested out his new found cooking skills by preparing a big Sunday dinner but earlier he had told Maureen he wasn't feeling well: he was planning to break up with her and he wasn't going to put either one of them through a traditional Sunday dinner first. She brought Chinese take-out but after she had set up the TV tables and opened the cartons of sesame noodles and cashew chicken, Brian found he actually could not eat.

"You're really not feeling well, are you?" she asked. "What's wrong?"

Brian shrugged and pulled a blanket over his lap. Now would be a good time to start, he thought: 'what's wrong' was a good way in. But as soon as he opened his mouth, he heard himself describing symptoms he did not have: headache, nausea, sore throat. As a medical student, Maureen offered to look at his throat but he shook his head no. Soon enough she would discover he was a coward, he didn't want her to know he was a liar, too. Still, she felt his head for the fever he did not have, tucked the blanket around his shoulders and neck anyway, and switched on the TV. While they watched a movie and Maureen ate the Chinese she'd brought, Brian tried to form the right words in his head. At every commercial, he sat up straighter, gathered his breath and his courage and opened his mouth to speak. Each time the movie resumed, he had said nothing.

When the movie was over, Maureen suggested they go to bed but Brian said he wasn't tired.

"But you're sick," she said, "you need to sleep."

"I'm not sick," Brian answered. Maureen looked at him. Then she stood up and looked down at him. He kept his head pointed toward his lap.

"Look at me," she said, and he did. She stared at him for several seconds and then went into the bedroom by herself.

In the morning when Brian got up from the couch and went to his room, Maureen was gone. He had no idea what time she had left. The uneaten Chinese food was still on the coffee table and the living room smelled of soy sauce and cold grease. Whenever Maureen left before Brian was up, she'd leave a little goodbye note by the coffeemaker. He did not even bother to look for a note he knew would not be there.

He should call her to explain, he thought, but the way she looked at him and the way she left made it pretty clear she didn't want to talk. Maybe it's what she wanted, too, Brian began to rationalize but he knew that wasn't true and as much as he wanted to end the relationship, he was not going to put the responsibility for what he'd done on an innocent Maureen. She had given up a lot to stay here in Miami with him but she had been sure her sacrifice was more of an investment: Brian had promised that, eventually, they would move back to Chicago. Now he at least wanted to call her and tell her he was sorry. But like so many things Brian truly believed he wanted to do, he postponed the call and decided to shower first. While getting dressed, Brian thought that maybe apologizing to Maureen would not be the best approach. He resolved to think it through more carefully while at work; he would call her tonight when he got home.

The moment Brian walked into the store on Monday morning, he saw an elderly white woman with a black chauffeur standing partially in and partially outside of Will's office. The woman was old and shriveled, skin swayed from her arms, which were flying out of her sleeveless dress as she ranted.

"Pins!" she yelled, "straight pins! The kind I used to use when I hemmed my own dresses as a girl. Pins!" The chauffeur was shaking his head, removing his official hat and running his hand across his head before putting the hat back in place. It was very hot in the store.

"Maam, please. Slow down," Will was saying.

"Slow down? Your pins might've slowed me down for good, young man. There were straight pins in my beans. Pins. Charles here was washing my beans and he found pins in them, in every one. Are you trying to kill me?"

Despite the fact that the woman was exaggerating—there were many beans in this pound without pins—she was perfectly justified in being irate: there were about a dozen beans that, when pinched, revealed long straight sewing pins.

Brian walked past them into Will's office and the two exchanged glances of helplessness. Nails in the lettuce. Glass in the broccoli. Now pins in the yellow wax beans. But although he was listening to Will and nodding his head—they offered this woman a year's worth of free groceries—his head was already back in produce.

The old woman turned down their offer and vowed never to set foot in The Crystal Market again; when she and her chauffeur left, Brian did not wait to talk with Will: he went immediately to the storeroom for latex gloves and then went out into the produce aisle. It was just beginning to occur to him that something was terribly wrong. At first, it had seemed like a coincidence; now it seemed like a conspiracy. While he was rubbing every potato—Idaho, creamer, purple, redskin, every single one of every single kind, looking for bumps, angles, points, protrusions—Will came up beside him.

"I don't understand this," Will said, and he seemed very sad. "What are we going to do?"

"I'm just going to have to keep a closer eye on things."

"Brian, be reasonable: you can't spend your whole career checking vegetables for glass. I'm going to call the police."

It had not occurred to Brian to involve the police; until the moment Will uttered the word, it had not occurred to Brian that what was taking place was a crime.

***

"Could someone be trying to ruin your business?" the Sergeant asked, "is there a lot of competition?" Both Will and Brian thought hard. The Crystal Market had been a neighborhood mainstay since Will opened it 30 years ago. Over the years, other small markets and specialty shops had come and gone but most had stayed; The Crystal Market enjoyed healthy congenial relationships with other shopkeepers, traded vendor secrets, advised on good and bad companies, even had meetings every three or four months to discuss neighborhood business. The shops that failed were too trendy; in this part of Miami, it was neighbors that counted.

While the Sergeant took notes, a young woman rushed in with a bleeding lip. "This peach," she screamed, "I bit into this peach and look." She extended the peach, which had the thin edge of a razor blade protruding from it. "Oh my God," she said, "I'm dying."

In what seemed like the amount of time it took for her to speak a dozen words, a crowd had formed. People hissed and gasped and demanded to know what was going on. The woman was screaming and rightfully so: she had taken a peach out of the bag on her way to her car and when she bit into it, it tore her bottom lip and produced blood. But, mercifully, the blade had only grazed the skin and although she was bleeding, she didn't even need stitches. Will was putting a tissue to the woman's lips and Brian was patting her on the shoulder with one hand and examining the peach with the other when the cop took the peach from Brian and said, "whoever did this was very careful: see where this blade is? The perpetrator made sure the person who ate this peach only got nicked."

The perpetrator? Will and Brian both felt their blood thin, their skin shrink back from their bones. Now they looked like father and son, with sweat forming at their temples and under their arms, with their hands moving back and forth at their sides. At the same time, each man put a sweaty palm through his hair. Neither knew what to do or say but it didn't matter: throughout the entire afternoon, no one who worked at The Crystal Market had a chance to say anything.

First, a woman appeared who had found a screw in her tomato, the sticker covering the point of entry. While she was still in Will's office, a grandfather and his grandson appeared; they were making their family's famous Eggplant Parmesan when they discovered pieces of lead from a mechanical pencil smoothly slipped inside the huge purple ovals. Around lunch time Mandy, a local caterer who had been shopping at the Crystal for ten years, discovered dark purple marbles amidst her concord grapes ("one of my guests almost swallowed one!" she screamed). And on Mandy's heels, Will's next door neighbor's mother-in-law came in; when she tried to slice through a green cabbage, her knife hit a series of thin, sharp metal plates. By noon, Will had no choice but to close the store.

Will and Brian and the rest of the staff met every morning for the month they were closed. The Crystal staff discussed possible theories but they couldn't come up with anything that made sense. They contacted other neighborhood stores but no one had had any situations like the ones they had experienced. Suppliers had no idea what could have happened: none of their other customers had complained. They went over charge receipts and house accounts, discussing every customer they could come up with to see if maybe that person could be capable of something like this. The danger lurked that they would become suspicious of one another. At the end of every session, they were at a loss to explain it, except to say that someone who they did not know or could not recognize had managed to sabotage the store without any of them noticing.

In the afternoons, they scoured the entire store, not just produce, for possible dangers. Butch and Miranda of the Fish Department poked their fingers into every filet. Augustus, George, Nellie and Eduardo turned over every single canned good to be sure no tampering had taken place, no puncture holes, no boccilism, no dents. Everything they found that seemed even slightly damaged, they threw out; they would not be taking their weekly truck load of food to the homeless shelters. All the wines and beers were checked. All the beef and poultry and pork was poked, prodded, and sniffed. Although the problem seemed to be confined to produce, no one was taking any chances. The bakery was completely disposed of and the bakers began again anew. In produce, Ruth discovered three more peaches with razor blades and Louise cut her finger on the blade of a paring knife that was laying between two stalks of rhubarb; they all tried to take the blame for the knife, everyone in produce thinking maybe they had left it there by accident. But no one could take the blame for razor blades.

At the end of the month, The Crystal Market reopened but with an extremely cautious and financially strapped staff: everyone was very nervous. Brian had spent the month planning for the reopening with Will; although they worked full days, Brian refused Will's offer of full pay and spent his evenings eating macaroni and cheese or peanut butter sandwiches and watching TV. He thought a lot about Dani during that month, too, wondering if he would ever see her again. He was sure she knew why the market had closed and he knew she must have found a new, safer place to buy her food. On a couple of occasions, he took a walk around the neighborhood hoping he'd pass her on the street or see her car.

Despite the fact that no "perpetrator" had been caught, employees of The Crystal Market believed that now that they were sure the store was in perfect condition, they could monitor every department. They vowed to be vigilant. Will hired half a dozen more employees, and a private security firm: cops in uniform and in plainclothes were placed strategically around the store, and they moved through it continuously.

Business was very slow at first: in fact, during the first week, there were whole days when no one was in the store but the people who worked there. And there were some mixed blessings: although somehow the local news had not aired the stories, word-of-mouth had clearly directed shoppers to other markets; and even though none of the injured customers had sued the store, those loyal people would never return. But Will placed ads in the local newspapers for great new buys at The Crystal Market. Little by little, business picked up. By the end of the fourth week of being re-opened, both Will and Brian felt some relief. The clientele was not as it used to be but people were coming in to shop and even some old customers—unharmed but still reluctant—were returning.

Every day Brian waited for Dani but she never came. The melodrama of his fantasies had long subsided: he knew if something terrible had happened, he would have heard. Now, when he thought of Dani, he just felt longing. And regret. Maureen had agreed to put their problems on hold until the trouble at the market had been resolved, but now he knew he had to tell her the truth. He called her and in his clumsy way, blurted out how he didn't want to leave Miami or The Crystal Market, how he wasn't ready to be married. When she asked him when he thought he might be ready to be married, he told her about Dani.

"But you don't even know that girl," Maureen said.

"I know, that's the point, I guess: I want to know her."

Maureen called him ridiculous. She reminded him how long they'd been together, how much they'd been through and asked if he really wanted to give all that up for three hours of breakfast. He tried to explain and he tried to apologize, too, but every time he got started, she interrupted him, alternating with memories, pleas to give it more time, guilt about her having to be in medical school here when she could have been at Northwestern, admonitions about what both of their families would say and, finally, insults.

"Asshole," she finally said, and hung up the phone.

"I care about you. I didn't want to hurt you," Brian winced as he heard himself relying on the old clichés, even though they were true. Maybe if he had never met Dani, he would want to marry Maureen. He didn't understand it so how could he make Maureen understand it? He placed the phone receiver in its cradle and slumped back on the couch. Now what? He tried to figure out how to feel. Even though he did feel terrible about how he'd shattered Maureen, he was surprised at how little remorse he felt about ending a relationship that had lasted almost nine years; he was even more surprised by how devastated he was about not being able to find the girl he barely knew. And maybe he shouldn't even try: something was obviously wrong with Dani after that last breakfast and, after all, she had not once tried to get a hold of him, at least not that he knew of. Had he been too self-absorbed? Should he have asked her to talk about her life? Was it the stuff about Maureen? He had no idea.

He got up, showered and went to work. He tried to concentrate on the store but it wasn't working. Finally, unable to think about much else than Dani, he talked about it with Will.

"Well, call the sister," Will declared, as if it was the simplest thing in the world.

"How?" Brian didn't even know Dani's sister's name.

"I don't know: how many Newmans can there be in the Mayor's office?"

*   *   *

Brian slowed down when he reached the corner of Dani's street; he could see her building. Although her sister had been very warm and gracious—she had given him their phone number, address and invited him to come by for a drink sometime—he was still uneasy about whether Dani would want to see him. Then he remembered how her sister recognized his name immediately and so freely gave out the information: that's what gave him the ultimate courage. In the end, he bought a bunch of sunflowers and decided he had nothing left to loose; if she wasn't home, he would leave them. There was a Crystal Market sticker on the cellophane; she would know.

Dani and her sister did not have curtains or blinds on their windows; when Brian walked up to the door of their building, he could see Dani lying on the couch reading a magazine. He thought about scraping all of his plans except the one where he put the flowers on her doorstep and left but then he was pressing the buzzer and from the corner of his eye, he could see her moving off the couch.

"Who is it?" she called from behind the door.

"It's Brian."

"Who?"

"Brian. From the market? The Crystal?"

Brian had that feeling that tells you you have just made an irrevocable mistake. After all the months of thinking and these last few days of nervous planning, he had picked the wrong approach. You don't just show up at someone's house. If he had been expecting someone—especially Dani—he would have showered, shaved, straightened up. But then the door opened.

"Brian," Dani said flatly.

"I'm sorry," he started, " I should have called. Your sister..."

"Yeah, I know: she said you called her." Dani turned, leaving an open space for him to walk through; although she didn't invite him in, he followed her. She seemed angry.

"So," she said, her teeth clenched, "sit down. I guess." She kept on walking through the living room.

"No, thanks, I'm only here for a minute. I just need to talk to you."

Dani stopped and turned to face him. Her face was stern but she also looked pale; he wondered if she was sick.

"Are you ok?" he asked.

She didn't answer but backed up to the couch and sunk down. Then she ran her hand through her hair and took a deep breath.

"Are you ok?" he asked again.

"I'm fine. Get it over with."

She didn't want him; "get it over with" made it all obvious to Brian now. She hadn't come back to the market because she didn't want to see him; now that he was here, she would listen to his pathetic tale and then she would tell him to get out.

"No, it's ok," he said, "I'll just go...I guess I should have called instead but I was afraid that you'd..."

"What?" Dani interrupted, "make a run for it?" Dani began to bite her lip and clap her hands together softly, as if she were applauding.

"Well, I don't know, maybe...I mean, you never came back to the market."

"Obviously," she said and shook her head.

"Why?"

"Why? You know why. Isn't that the reason you're here?"

"Because of the glass and stuff in the vegetables?" he asked.

"Of course." Dani was still clapping her hands together and now she was tapping her feet.

"Yeah, but I thought you would have heard that we got that all cleared up and then you would come back. You know, the whole time that was going on I never saw you and I kept thinking that maybe you ate something from the market with nails or glass in it and that something happened to you and..."

Dani sat upright and leaned over her knees. "Wait a minute: you thought that I...you got that all cleared up? How?"

"We closed down, we went through the whole store, we hired detectives, we did everything we could do. We've been open for a while now and so far, so good."

"So far, so good? You hired detectives? Did they...did they figure out who did it?"

"No. We don't know what happened. We're just really glad no one got seriously hurt."

Dani sank back into the couch. Brian was staring at her but she wouldn't look up. At first, he thought she was going to cry but then very slowly, a small grin formed on her mouth. She pulled her legs up Indian-style and then dropped her head to her chest. When she finally looked up, she was smiling.

"So, then, what *are* you doing here?"

"I need to talk to you."

"About what?" Now she was laughing.

Brian sat down in a chair beside the couch and even though he thought Dani was laughing at him, he still managed to say all the things he'd been thinking about saying for months. He told her about how he felt when they were together and how he felt when they were apart; he told her how stupid he thought he'd been, how selfish; he told her he'd broken up with Maureen and that she'd moved back home.

"But not before telling me what an asshole I was," Brian said, "and I was. Look, Dani, I'm sorry. I'm don't know what your situation is...we don't really even know each other, but I just wanted to come over here and tell you these things I should have told you a long time ago. And I was thinking maybe if you wanted to, we could do something...like go to a movie or out for dinner."

"So you broke up with Maureen?" Dani said, standing up. "I should put those flowers in water," she said, taking the bouquet of sunflowers from his lap. "Do you want some tea?"

"Tea?" Brian said, surprised at the change but fearful of ruining it. "Sure. Tea would be great."

"Good. Come in the kitchen with me while I make it."

The kitchen would have been a typical urban apartment kitchen with standard stove and refrigerator, deep ceramic sink, bad lighting. There were wire baskets hanging from various places, all filled with tomatoes, peaches, eggplants and cabbage. On the counter was a coffee pot, tea-maker, and baskets of coffee and tea. The refrigerator door was covered with photos, recipes, newspaper articles, magnets from a local dry cleaner and a gym. But what distinguished it was Dani's drafting board and easel taking up the far corner, along with all her supplies: pens, pencils with the boxes of thin lead, glue and rubber cement, razors and Exacto knives, paint brushes, watercolors, thin metal plates for weighting paper down. On a table in the corner was a piece Dani was working on; she saw him see it.

"Oh," she said quickly, "don't look at that: it's not even good."

"What is it," he asked, noting the materials, broken green glass, dried leaves from her ficus tree, some red and purple marbles, wine labels.

"It's a picture frame. I got a commission from a wine

shop on Biscayne; when it's done, it's going to look like a grape vine. But it's stupid. Here, come on: the tea's ready."

Brain went to the table and sat down; he was relieved by the smell of the green tea, the kind they drank together at Berries.

"Beautiful," Brian said, taking a deep sip. "So how did you think it all up anyway?"

"Think what all up?" Dani said too quickly, her sip of tea slipping from her lips to the table.

"The picture frame. To make it out of old wine bottles and labels...and marbles for grapes."

"Oh, well, you know...I've had a lot of time on my hands."

Phyllis

...sharing food with another human being
is an intimate act that should not be indulged
in lightly.

M.F.K. Fisher, The Art of Eating

Phyllis Whitman is throwing a party. A cocktail party, with drinks (and champagne) and hors d'oeuvres. She's made nearly everything herself, down to the crackers and breadsticks. Two days ago, her husband Roger left for a business trip, the first one in nearly a year; the second his car pulled out of the drive, Phyllis threw on sweatpants and a t-shirt, dark sunglasses and her daughter's old high school softball cap, and ran to Epicure, the gourmet grocery on Alton Road.

Very slowly, she walked up and down every aisle, carefully committing to memory Epicure's specialty items—their baked brie, Thai peanut chicken bites, the spellbinding vegetable platters. Then with these images in her mind, she shopped methodically: high-end markets like Epicure were like recipes, good only for ideas and ingredients.

Phyllis picked up and then put down packages of mushrooms whose contents didn't seem to be all the same size. She squeezed individual grapes to be sure all the members of the clusters were firm. She asked the man behind the fish counter to see several pieces of salmon and unabashedly poked them until she found one whose flesh resisted her prodding. Phyllis pulled apart endive leaves, snapped pea pods, insisted on a fresh flat of eggs from the cooler in the back and drove clerks and butchers and stock boys to distraction. She saw store employees rolling their eyes at her, and at each other because of her, but she didn't care: she was giving a party and everything had to be perfect.

Right now, Phyllis is in the crawl space beneath her big

house, searching the musty dank storage areas for a certain set of stainless steel toothpicks with tiny shrimps welded to the top that she is certain she received as a wedding gift some thirty-five years ago.

Cut to the kitchen, even though she is not there. It is immaculate and gleaming, scrubbed, polished and predominately silver-gray. The stove and refrigerator, counters and wine cooler are all stainless steel; the wood is pine. Someone once remarked that Phyllis had redone her kitchen in her own image: at 57, she has let her hair go natural gray, though you can see some remnants of blonde when she sweeps it up into a modernized version of what used to be called the French Twist. Phyllis is lightly tanned, angular, and just barely shows lines in her face and on her hands. She is lucky because she no longer takes very good care of herself.

On the stainless counter top is a huge, flat woven basket filled with her homemade breadsticks and crackers; each item is laid out in a column, each item in each column the exact same size as the items preceding and following it. Phyllis has made pumpernickel rounds, water crackers, sesame sticks and lavosh. With these she will serve a full round brie with a caramelized top, thin slivers of apple and almonds, and dots of fresh currants (more complicated than the one the chefs at Epicure displayed but still inspired by them); she also has a salmon mousse, having poached and flaked the salmon herself first. The mousse is decorated with cucumber slices, capers, sprigs of fresh dill and triangles of lemon.

These two trays are in the refrigerator next to the superb "make-your-own-caviar" tray. Phyllis is a bit worried about this tray since the moment one of her guests indulges, the symmetry will be destroyed. Still, she figures that she will be able to keep an eye on it, nonchalantly walk to the table as if she were going to eat (which she would not) and use a silver cocktail knife to reconfigure her design. The tray was created with a circular motif: large outer circle of chopped egg white; next, circle of chopped egg yolk. Then, as you move into the center, circles of capers, minutely diced black olives, an undulating wave of sour cream, black caviar, red caviar, golden caviar and in the middle, finely chopped red onion. These caviar canapés go particularly well with the homemade lavosh.

There is also an enormous crystal bowl (not a wedding gift; Phyllis bought this for herself) full of jumbo steamed shrimp, with the tails on. These need no garnish as in and of themselves, they are magnificent. But Phyllis has made two dipping sauces: a traditional cocktail type with extra horseradish, and an herb-infused remoulade.

Finally, the refrigerator also houses a tray of all perfectly round items; this is set-up like a necklace from Henry Winston; in fact, Phyllis used an advertisement of a multi-layered Winston necklace for her inspiration. There are small sweet grape tomatoes, button mushrooms, dark Greek olives, steamed and marinated miniature brussel sprouts, boiled and salted new potatoes, steamed and dressed young purple and golden beets, all in decreasing semi-circles on a brightly polished silver tray.

If we were to open the freezer, side by side with the refrigerator and just as large, we would find several trays ready to go into the oven half an hour before the guests are due to arrive. There are miniature Quiche Lorraines, tiny duck eggrolls, discs of polenta topped with bits of sun-dried tomato, squares of Spanikopita, skewers of already-sauteed chicken satay, and beef roulades filled with bacon, pickles and mustard. Sauces, of course, are ready to be paired with each item.

Phyllis could afford to buy an entire restaurant let alone hire a caterer. She did have desserts brought in because she is no longer interested in sweets. She is also not interested in cleaning, so she has hired servers and cleaners, and a firm that brings alcohol and mixers and bartends. In the last year, Phyllis has taken a liking to martinis.

Which brings us back to Phyllis in the crawl space. A box of dusty cordial glasses reminds her that she would like a drink, though she has not yet found what she crawled down here for. But she must hurry: within an hour, all of the hired help will appear and an hour after that, Roger will be home from his trip; Phyllis must be dressed before they all arrive. Since we left her in the crawl space, she has found a variety of items she forgot she owned and they have produced a range of emotions, all of which she is trying to quell: she nearly laughs when a box she opens contains a papier mache globe Laurel had made in sixth grade, lopsided and utterly inaccurate in terms of geography. But at least she got France right. Phyllis sees the glass punch bowl Roger's grandmother had given them when they married. She discovers two hats she wore on her honeymoon, a set of plastic iced tea glasses, her old tennis racket and before she can help it, she uncovers a box with tart pans, berry pitters, rolling pins, pastry cutters—all of her old baking supplies—including the two stained cookie sheets she could not bring herself to clean. It is at that moment, when she turns too quickly to leave, that she spots a little box wedged beside a bigger box and finds the shrimp picks.

By the time Phyllis gets upstairs, checks all the trays again, rearranges a few groups of grapes in the fruit bowl (this is another masterpiece: a bowl of grapes—green, red, purple and black, appearing to be whole strands but actually snipped with kitchen shears into manageable individual clumps), polishes the shrimp-picks and sticks them strategically into the shrimps, it is time to get dressed. She showers quickly, talcolms, sweeps her hair up into the twist and secures it with an antique diamond hairclip, applies the smallest amount of charcoal eyeliner and pink lipgloss, a discrete pair of diamond stud earrings, and slips on her gunmetal sleeveless sheath—a perfect hostess dress because it is elegant but allows one to move around—she has precisely four minutes before the workers will arrive.

Maria is already there and has been there since she lives in the small garage apartment attached to the Whitman home; when Phyllis comes downstairs, Maria is wearing the black dress and white apron that now designates her a member of the kitchen and she is standing at the door waiting for the workers to show up. When they do, they begin to take over the house so Phyllis sits on the porch sipping the martini Maria has prepared for her because it makes her too nervous to watch strangers so familiar in her own home. When Roger gets home, he will have to change, and then mix himself a drink (he is particular about his martinis), and get ready to greet their guests.

As usual, the guest list had been traumatic to assemble. If you invited the Holcombs, which you wanted since they were such good company, then you really had to invite the Baxters, though Roger could not stand Henry Baxter. He was a snob, the kind of man who took over a conversation the moment he entered it. But Phyllis knows that Roger will not have to worry because there will be so many people to talk with, he need not get into even one small conversation with the pompous Henry Baxter.

They had also invited the Ringleys and the McCulloughs, who were related by marriage, Sylvia and Cornelia being sisters a year apart. Phyllis did not know how Cornelia could stand being called "Corny" (though she thought "Sylvie" a sweet nickname) but Corny was tall, square, hearty and very confident. Corny and Bennett's daughter Veronica had grown up with Laurel; they had been good friends, playing tennis together on weekends at the country club, learning how to bake in Phyllis's kitchen, and sometimes even sharing clothes. Laurel would have liked seeing Veronica's parents again.

Then there was the country club group who by virtue of their position in the club got invited to any party given by any member: Morgans (yes, related), Lynchs, Millers, Ritenauers, Brundlows, Brownings (no, not related to the poets, not even distantly), Nelsons and Jackmans.

Despite the fact that Phyllis doesn't really even like most of this latter group, they made for excellent party fare because they knew everyone, all the gossip and all the late-breaking club and social news. And as an added bonus, they spread the word around their circle when a party was exceptional, as Phyllis believes hers will be. As they had always been: over the years, Phyllis had prided herself in the high level of her get-togethers, in the way people who were invited swooned and people who weren't pulled their chairs up to hers at the club pool, "just to chat."

Roger does not know about the party but she knows he will be pleasantly surprised, as he used to be, when he sees that Phyllis has laid his clothes out neatly on the bed so that when he gets home, all he will have to do is shower, shave, powder and slip on his soft charcoal grey trousers and lighter grey jersey. Roger appreciated Phyllis's quiet thoughtfulness; a typically taciturn New Englander who had come to Miami in his early twenties and made millions in the banking industry, he never adopted Miami's flair for the exuberant, the extravagant, the brash. For this, Phyllis has always been grateful and relieved. Roger and Phyllis have a lovely, if quiet, marriage; without a lot of talking, they understand each other.

Actually, they had talked a lot during most of their years together. In fact, the night they met, on a flight which was Roger's eight or ninth trip to Hong Kong and Phyllis's very first time as a flight attendant in First Class on an overseas flight, they had been downright chatty. Over the eternal expanse of the Pacific, they traded most of the important information: Phyllis, who lived outside of Ft. Lauderdale, was an ex-art student from a small town in Georgia and Roger was a bachelor who avoided the high life in Miami; Phyllis had no family but her widowed mother who came on the bus from Rome, Georgia, to visit her daughter every year at Christmas and Roger's parents were deceased but he had a sister who lived with her husband and two children in London; neither of them saw their families much or dated much but both of them had subscriptions to **The New Yorker** which they had no problem keeping up with, local Sunday afternoon symphony performances and the catalogue from the Met; each had a favorite neighborhood breakfast café where whenever their schedules permitted, they had morning coffee and indulged in pancakes or waffles or sticky muffins—anything warm and sweet. When the plane landed, Phyllis was urgently trying to think of something else to say to Roger Whitman, something that would prolong their conversation, when he asked her if she'd like to go and have some authentic Chinese dinner.

Roger took her to a little out of the way Chinese restaurant where they sat next to each other in a booth for two instead of across from one another like everyone else, and talked all night. He fed her fried squid and tiny duck dumplings dipped in cherry sauce. When he dropped her off in the hotel lobby, he kissed her for a long time in front of anyone who happened to be walking by; he promised to call her when he got back to the States. She believed him because she wanted to, a trait she has never been able to outgrow. In spite of the fact that Phyllis believed Roger Whitman was too much—too rich, too handsome, too confident, too funny, too easy to talk to—she was still able to transform the reality into a fantasy that would end with happily ever after. At least until she got up into her room. At the sink, washing her face in the cold bathroom, Phyllis saw who she was: an ordinary, young and still somewhat silly girl who had chosen flying because she couldn't face staying in one place after her studio art professors said they could not recommend her to graduate school. "You don't take enough risks," one said during her senior thesis presentation, and the other concurred: "Maybe you should be an art teacher: I've known many a great teacher who was not a great artist."

That night in Hong Kong, Phyllis had a hard time falling asleep. She alternated between the dream she tried to force herself to have—the one where her professors were wrong and she proved it, painting anyway because she couldn't not paint and being discovered as a great talent—and the one she could not help but having, where she stayed in Hong Kong, went to the building where Roger Whitman was having his meeting, and he proposed.

When she woke up in the morning, it was with a sick

headache from fatigue and too much wine. The rich business-man was gone; she was a flight attendant who hadn't touched a paint brush in three years and who was scheduled back in Coach for the return flight. The fortune cookie she had snuck out of the restaurant Mr. Roger Whitman had whisked her to had been crushed under her fitful sleep, just beneath the thin hotel pillow.

Bleary eyed and slow with despair, Phyllis still made it to her flight early that morning. The first thing she did after the plane achieved cruising altitude was to spill hot coffee onto a passenger in a white business suit: the woman shrieked and made such a scene that everyone on the plane knew what had hap-pened and Phyllis, over profuse apologies and her address for the dry-cleaning bill, knew that when she got home she would have to find another job. This wasn't the first time she'd caused some kind of catastrophe for a passenger but judging from the look on the senior flight attendant's face, she knew it would be the last. She wondered what sort of graceful girl was now doing a perfect job of serving hot coffee to Roger Whitman at his busi-ness meeting.

After the spilled coffee fiasco, it seemed to Phyllis to take an eternity to get to the last 12 rows of the plane. She pushed the drink cart down the narrow aisle, slowly making her way to the very back, the place where she had started and where when she was done mixing Bloody Marys and pouring coffee and fill-ing bottles with apple juice for crying babies, she thought she could sit down for five minutes before preparing the breakfast cart. Her head still hurt and despair made her more tired than usual. But this particular drink service took much longer than the standard service: she ran out of coffee, few people had the right change for their Mimosas, and a youngish man with a spiky hair cut who looked as though he couldn't have been more than twenty spent an inordinately long time complaining that his brand of Scotch, one Phyllis could not find, was always available on these flights. Finally, she got to row 62, knowing she had time only to turn around and start all over again, this time with the breakfast choices—"Omelette or French Toast?"—when Roger Whitman stuck his hand out from Seat 62 A and said, "If you promise not to spill anything on me, I might have a new job for you."

Roger and Phyllis married beautifully—her mother actually fainted when she walked into the club where the reception was held but revived with some sips of champagne and the assurance that Roger had already paid for the entire affair—and honeymooned in Barbados, a place they visited every year for the duration of their 35 year marriage. They only had one child, Laurel, who was almost too good to be true: not only was she beautiful, with Phyllis's blonde hair and gentle features and Roger's wide white smile, and gifted in track & field, horseback riding and art, she was smart enough to get into Williams and a dutiful, fun-to-be-with daughter who actually enjoyed spending time with her parents. Much of the Whitman's house was dotted with framed pictures of the trio—Phyllis, Roger and Laurel—camping on their safari in Africa, trekking in Nepal, snorkeling in Eleuthra, kidding around with the pool guys in Barbados, bundled up in down in Alaska, sweating in Brazil, even just cooking hot dogs in their own backyard. Now as Phyllis sits on her porch, sipping her second martini and looking forward to the compliments she will graciously accept when guests comment on how beautifully her daughter photographs, she realizes that the whirlwind cooking—all of that work in just two days—and all of this remembering has made her very tired.

Maria comes to the porch and asks Mrs. Whitman if it is too early to put the trays of hot hors d'oeuvres into the oven. Phyllis looks at her watch; it is 6:30 and the party is supposed to start at 7:30. Better wait a few minutes, she says, no one will show up on time. Roger is not yet home. Better to wait. Phyllis has become very good at waiting. Laurel went off to Paris for a two-year graduate program in Art History at the Louvre and Phyllis has become expert at waiting for letters, phone calls, flight information and homecomings. Phyllis could now wait for hors

Diane Goodman

d'oeuvres to go into the oven.

In her concern over this party, which somehow seems more important than the last few she has given, Phyllis had written to Laurel three weeks ago, outright asking her daughter for confirmation about the menu, guest list, and music choices. The party held such promise that Phyllis had a sneaking suspicion perhaps Laurel would come home to attend it, as a surprise. Laurel has not been home in nearly a year. Phyllis checks her watch as if it is a calendar confirming this fact and notices that Roger should be home by now. Then an odd but exhilarating idea consumes her: maybe Roger is late because he is secretly picking Laurel up at the airport?

The speculation seems so plausible that Phyllis finishes her martini, sets the glass down on the porch table and goes upstairs to check Laurel's old room. Although Laurel has been out of college for two years, Phyllis has kept the room exactly as it was during Laurel's childhood. All through college when Laurel had come home for holidays and summer vacations, Phyllis would insist on preserving her daughter's childhood ritual of being tucked in and read to by her mother. By the time Laurel was a senior, Phyllis was reading parts of the books Laurel was studying for her Honors courses: History of Art, Heminway's **A Farewell to Arms**, Camille Paglia (which Phyllis didn't really like or understand but Laurel seemed grafted to).

Everything is in order in Laurel's room, as always. The bed is made with the brightly patterned Marimeko spread that Laurel had picked out the summer before she left for France. The walls sport standard reproductions of Picasso and Pissaro, and one framed authentic Modigliani, a rendering of a sad, long-faced, intensely beautiful woman in red. Above Laurel's bed is the painting of a garden that Phyllis and her daughter had done together during four weeks of one summer when Laurel, after a rock-climbing spill, had been laid up with a broken leg. The memory threatens to break Phyllis so she turns to all of the recipes they had invented together—butterscotch brownies, raspberry-blueberry cobbler for the Fourth of July, Tarte Tatin (in preparation for Laurel's trip to France), lemon mousse, peach shortcake—that are printed out in Laurel's calligraphy and tucked into the edges of Laurel's mirror. When Laurel left for France, she made sure she and her mother both had calligraphied copies of these recipes so that they could bake separately and imagine eating together. At the airport, during a teary goodbye, Phyllis and Laurel had made a pact: if the Art History degree didn't work out, mother and daughter would go into the bakery business together. When Laurel took one last trip to the bathroom before boarding the plane, Phyllis stuck a plastic bag of almond cookies—shaped like half moons and stars and dusted with sparkly vanilla sugar—into the outside pocket of her daughter's carry-on bag. Nothing short of the moon and the stars for my girl, she thought, imagining her daughter's tears on the plane being subdued by the fragrant cookies they had baked together the night before.

All of Laurel's junior high and high school books are alphabetized along the shelves (this had taken Phyllis an entire weekend to organize); her little trinkets and horseback riding trophies and basketball medals are dustless and shiny and lined up on a white shelf. Framed family pictures, some duplicates from around the house, cover much of the available space on Laurel's dresser and desk.

I wish she could come home, Phyllis thinks, closing the door to her daughter's room, knowing that Laurel cannot possibly come home but still believing she might, and heading back down to the porch.

Phyllis stops in the kitchen. She doesn't want to intrude on the workers but she is worried that they might not take real care with the trays, that they might overcook the duck egg rolls. But when Phyllis looks into her kitchen, she sees that Maria has everything under control; Maria tells Phyllis that they have, in fact, just now put a few trays of hors d'oeuvres in the oven. The two bars—one in the living room and one on the pool patio—

are open and bowls of cashews, roasted almonds, olives and marinated mozzarella balls are placed strategically around the house. As soon as guests arrive, Maria says they will be directed to the bars and tables of preliminary snacks, and the workers will then begin to set up the various tables throughout the house.

Don't worry, Maria assures Phyllis.

Thank you, Maria, Phyllis replies, with complete faith in this woman who is so efficient, so professional, so ready to tackle any unforeseen glitch.

When Phyllis opens the front door and emerges onto the porch, she is immediately overcome by a jolt of disappointment. Roger is sitting in her chair, just setting down her martini glass, which Maria must have replaced and from which he has obviously taken a few long sips.

Hello, darling, she says: he is not driving home from the airport with a thrilled Laurel, getting ready to surprise her mother with an almost completely unexpected visit. Well, she says to her husband, now you know: we are having another party. Aren't you going to get dressed?

Sit down, sweetheart, Roger says. Here: finish your drink: I'll go fix myself one.

There's a bartender, Phyllis says brightly, there are two, in fact. They'll make you a drink.

You know I like to stir my own, he replies, smiling and walking back into the house frowning, making sure he has closed the screen door quietly behind him. Oh well, thinks Phyllis, sipping her drink and thinking she might have time for one more before the guests arrive, especially since Roger has had about a third of this second one (she would not have a single drink while the party is taking place). In spite of her hopes, she knew Laurel would not be coming home. Sometimes her fantasies of Laurel's homecoming end up spoken out loud to Roger, and now she wonders if she will tell him about this most recent one.

Phyllis sips her martini slowly and when she has only one small sip left, she is about to get up and get one more when

Maria comes out and announces that everything is ready. She asks Mrs. Whitman if she'd like another drink.

Please, Phyllis says to the lovely Maria, who always makes sure all of Phyllis's efforts are timed well and presented perfectly.

Of course, Maria says, And by the way, Mrs. Whitman? Your food is absolutely stunning.

Thank you, dear, Phyllis replies. She is touched by the word "stunning."

Roger returns to the porch in the clothes Phyllis has set out for him, even though he had gone upstairs to put on gym shorts and a t-shirt. He has combed his hair and has a chilled martini of his own in his hand. He is about to suggest that his wife have another when Maria appears with Phyllis's fourth drink. Phyllis takes the drink and looks into its clarity before taking her first cool sip.

Should we go in and see if everything is in order? Phyllis asks her husband.

No, dear, he says, calmly, I think Maria is ready.

It's already 7:30, she observes.

Well, he says, then perhaps we should have a snack— taste some of the wonderful food you have prepared—before the guests arrive?

Oh, you know our friends, Phyllis says with a little laugh, they always come fashionably late. Let's just wait here: I don't want to disrupt the trays.

Well, how about another drink then? he suggests, seeing that his wife, his elegant stately wife who believes in the inconceivable and acts on the impossible as if it were a mere commonplace of their lives now, has nearly finished her fourth martini in the time it has taken them to have this short strained exchange.

Yes, Phyllis says, one more would be nice before all the hubbub begins.

You look beautiful, Roger says, bending down to kiss Phyllis, first on the top of her head and then down to her cheek, longer and with some force.

Thank you, dear, she says. She looks up into her husband's eyes, dark brown and full with the familiar concern she constantly misreads and says, Don't worry, Roger: the party will be lovely. And then she says, You know, darling, when you were late? I was carrying this funny fantasy that you were at the airport picking up Laurel, that she had gotten my letter about this party and was going to come home and surprise me.

You wrote to Laurel? Roger asks, his voice cracking with the news he always hopes not to hear again. Things had been going so well, or so he thought: that's why he had taken the risk and gone on this short business trip.

Yes, of course. I wrote to tell her about the party; I told her what I was going to make, the guest list, how I knew Morgans would stop in their tracks when they saw Nelsons here but wouldn't say anything, of course, because after all, what could they say? It's not the Nelsons' fault Kip dropped Ellie Morgan for that dancer on the Beach. I thought maybe the gossip would compel her home. Wasn't that silly?

She is home, Roger says, smoothing an errant strand of his wife's upswept silver hair back behind her ear. She is always home now, he thinks, swallowing a hard gulp of gin and spit and tears for his only child who was killed in a mountain climbing accident in the Pyrenees just before beginning her second year of graduate study in Art History at the Louvre.

Yes, of course, Phyllis replies. Now, what about that last drink? Before our guests arrive?

Roger nods, picks up Phyllis's empty glass and goes inside the house to talk to Maria.

When Laurel was in grade school, she used to help Maria clean the house, weed the garden and set canapés on trays when the Whitmans entertained. In Maria, Laurel had a live-in Spanish tutor, a cover for her high-school late nights out, an endlessly patient confidante and a co-conspirator in her mother's marathon baking extravaganzas, events that Laurel tolerated because she loved her mother but that also tested her teenage patience.

Every year for Christmas, Laurel gave Maria a handmade Christmas ornament and then a recipe for a dessert, printed out in calligraphy, half sincere and half tongue-in-cheek. We have to humor Mamma, Laurel would say, and try not to get too fat or too bored in the process. Your mamma worships you, Maria would scold; if only she knew...And they would laugh at their secrets, their risks, and the sincere authentic love each one had for Phyllis.

Now, Mr. Whitman? Maria asks and Roger nods his head. Maria shakes hers while instructing the hired staff, who have worked the Whitman parties before, to begin packing up and freezing all of the food Phyllis has spent two days preparing for guests who had never been invited. They will have to find a way to fit it inside the freezer that contains countless similar trays. Take some for yourself, he tells Maria, and she hugs him in thanks and in sympathy: Maria has been with the Whitman's for thirty years: she was just a girl when she started working for them as a housekeeper; when Laurel was born, she became a nanny and then a cook and then a girlfriend. Now she is a nurse.

Roger mixes himself a double martini and one with an extra shot for his wife, because he wants them both to be able to sleep. Soon. He pays the catering and bar bills with checks and then walks around the house giving every single worker a hundred dollar bill for their time and effort. The money is stored in the safe he has hidden under his desk. The safe contains cash, his mother's estate jewels, Laurel's college diploma and death certificate, instructions that will take care of Maria for the rest of her life, and very specific instructions for his lawyer in the unlikely event that he should die before his sweet, fragile, incomprehensible wife.

Then he returns to the porch with drinks and two plates that hold a sampling of all of the hors d'oeuvres, of all of the beautiful cared-for food that Maria will defrost for them to eat in bits and pieces over however many years together they have left.

Shiva

It was a carnal knife that let
Red Riding Hood out like a poppy,
quite alive from the kingdom of the belly.
And grandmother too
still waiting for cakes and wine.
The wolf, they decided, was too mean
to be simply shot so they filled his belly
with large stones and sewed him up.
He was as heavy as a cemetary
and when he woke up and tried to run off
he fell over dead. Killed by his own weight.
Many a deception ends on such a note.

Anne Sexton, Transformations
(Red Riding Hood)

Every time I tie this stupid sari around my waist, it slips down. It's one thing if I am only carrying a small tray of tea or drinks, or one dish and some rice, but when I have to use both hands to bring the food, I can feel the sari slipping down to my hips. So far, I have managed to get to my tables and set the food down before the damn thing just falls off. So far.

I like this job better than the last one I had so I try to tie the sari really tightly, but the tying and re-tying takes time away from my tables. I have already lost one job I loved for being too slow. It's not a traditional sari, though it looks like one; here at The Shiva Indian Restaurant, we wear skirts that look like saris and our own white or peach-colored t-shirts on top. There is a lot of fabric for the skirt and the Sahas don't seem to mind if my midriff shows. I would prefer it didn't; a bulge of skin threatens to skim the top and look disgusting but there doesn't seem to be anything I can do. I suck and suck my stomach in but then the sari slips down further anyway; it doesn't seem to matter that I have the smallest sari in the restaurant and no matter how big my shirts are, the sari falls below their hems.

Table Four has ordered the Vegetarian Platter. There is a bowl of Aloo Ghobi, a bowl of Paneer, a bowl of dark green and orange vegetable curry with raisins and nuts, a ramekin of the yogurt-cucumber-white pepper sauce called Raita, and big circles of steamy Nan. All of the bowls are placed on a wide silver tray. The smell of the food makes me so hungry that I slip five fennel seeds into my mouth. I tighten the sari, lift the tray with both hands and hope for the best.

I am always hungry here, which is one of the biggest differences between this job and the one I had at the Bagel Factory. The smell of boiling bagel dough used to make me sick. One of my tasks, at least when I first worked there, was to lift the bagels out of the milky water and take them to the bakers. The wet unbaked bagels were sticky and slimy. The whole time I worked at the Bagel Factory, I used to have this dream. I was a starving baby cradled in my mother's lap. She had long soothing hair that covered my eyes when she leaned over to give me a bottle I thought was filled with warm milk; when the hot cloudy bagel water filled my mouth, my cries got caught in it as it ran down my throat and my tears dissolved in my mother's red hair.

In the Bagel Factory kitchen, the bakers would bake the bagels off, then and salt or seed the ones requiring salting or seeding; other ones had blueberries or chocolate chips or shredded cheese or raisins in them. Although I wanted to get out of the kitchen as soon as I had dropped off the boiled dough, the idea of these thick bagels filled with fruits or sweets, the way the bagels with blueberries would turn a green color and the way the cheese would harden like clipped fingernails compelled me to stay and watch and ask questions. Who came up with these recipes? How could people eat this kind of food? What was the appeal?

Then Mrs. Feinberg took me out of the kitchen and put me behind the counter but that was worse. Oily lox, whitefish spread, chopped liver, vegetable cream cheese. I couldn't fill an order without my throat closing from the idea that someone was actually going to swallow these things; often, I had to take a few seconds to breathe again before opening the refrigerated case and releasing the smells. I fantasized customers who would request only coffee or diet coke. It took me a long time to fill orders; sometimes, it occurred to me that when customers saw me stick the spatula into the mysterious containers whose contents didn't look anything like what the item cards said—the egg salad was nearly green from parsley and the low-fat tuna fish was actually pink—and realized that that mess was going on their bagel, they would change their minds. When they didn't, I tried very hard to smile and hide my fear when I handed over the paper-wrapped bagels oozing with fishy spreads or organ meat that had been cooked and mashed into a gray mud. But some people complained.

Eventually, Mrs. Feinberg said she had to let me go; it wasn't good for her customers to see me gag as I made their sandwiches. I protested a little because I thought I was trying very hard to act pleasant, and it was a lot harder for me than it was for the customers. But Mrs. Feinberg had made up her mind.

"Aren't you Jewish?" she asked me, when I was returning my Bagel Factory smock to the storeroom.

"Yes," I said, not understanding what that had to do with my performance.

"Didn't you grow up eating bagels?" she wanted to know, but I just shook my head. The truth is I did grow up around bagels; I just didn't eat any of them.

Across the street from the house I grew up in was a place called Amster Bagels. When my brother was little, about eight or nine, he and his friends would sneak into the back; Mr. Amster always left that door open because the massive ovens made the kitchen unbearably hot. Freddy and his friends would take as many bagels as they could get, steaming and crunchy, right off the baking trays. I'd be in the front of the store creating a diversion for them; I'd have a dollar or two in my hand and I'd walk back and forth in front of the case, eyeing the water bagels, egg bagels, poppy or sesame seed, as if I was trying to decide which ones I wanted to buy. When I saw Freddy and his pals running back into our house, I'd say "Never mind" to Mr. Amster and walk out.

Then I'd go home and continue babysitting for the little bagel thieves. I am five years older than my brother. I drank a lot of Cokes and pulled pepperonis off the pizzas our mother brought home for us, but I never ate a single bagel.

Still, Amster's was an important place for me. There was a ladder next to the open kitchen door. Sometimes when my mother was home, she would get really mad at me and Freddy. We never knew why. Sometimes we'd say something we didn't know was wrong or sometimes we wouldn't say anything, but either way she'd smack us. I remember never knowing how I was bad because if I had known, I would have stopped doing whatever it was that made her suddenly stop polishing her nails or paying the bills and snap her lips together as if she was afraid she was going to bite us. Then I'd rush in front of Freddy but she'd just slap my face to get me out of the way and then slap him. We were skinny and fast and although her rage was unpredictable, we grew up devising ways to stay clear of or get away from her. But sometimes she'd catch us off guard and sneak up behind us while we were lying on the den floor, watching TV; then, she'd slap us both at the same time, one with each hand. When she'd turn to call our father who lived about three blocks away, we ran. By the time we saw his Chevy Impala pull up in front of our house, we'd be on the roof of Amster's Bagels, breathing in the doughy air and laughing at how stupid our parents were. But most of the time, I have to admit, I'd be crying, too, partly out of helplessness and defeat and partly because my mother packed a punch. Freddy never cried and he always wiped the blood off my lip with his t-shirt sleeve. It's funny: I remember streaks of my blood on the long-sleeved Dallas Cowboys shirt that he often wore as pajamas and then as regular clothes for days in a row. I also remember feeling sleepy up there on Amster's roof and liking the way the warm smell of those bagels baking held me still. But all that changed when I grew up.

The Shiva Indian Restaurant where I now work is full of the most extraordinary smells. The spices, the Tandoor, the bubbling curries, the fragrant rices. There are five kinds of Nan: plain, one filled with eggplant and cumin, one packed with buttery mashed potatoes, one fried with garlic, one with the creamy spinach. I am a vegetarian but here at Shiva's, I am tempted to sample the lamb, simmered with green lentils, spices and tomatoes. Often when I am working, I suddenly realize that serving this beautiful food makes me feel as though I am starving, brings deep pulsing pains into my chest and stomach. When that happens, I know exactly what to do. I make my way to the front of the restaurant, to the foyer where customers stand sipping wine and waiting for their tables under the wise smirk of the life-size statue of the Dancing Shiva. My first day on the job here, Mr. Saha took me to this statue and explained Shiva, the Hindu deity who represents destruction. Shiva works miracles when you understand that you can't be restored without being destroyed first; but you have to concentrate and be remorseful. So when I think I am going to faint if I don't stick my hand into a steaming bowl of curry and push the food into my mouth, I go and stand in front of Shiva. I close my eyes and I repent; I understand that my pain is my penance. *The Dancing Shiva holds a spiritual light that burns away the veil of illusion*, Mr. Saha told me; my hunger is an illusion and I am truly sorry. The miracle takes only seconds. Then I can get back to work.

It's not that I couldn't eat something if I wanted to; I could. The whole restaurant staff is like part of the Saha's extended family and they feed us all. But the employee meal is served before every shift and one thing or another always keeps me from getting here before my shift starts. Not that I am ever late—I'm not—but everyday I think I'm going to show up at 4:45 and eat from the platter of Samosas or have a bowl of Mulligatawny soup, and the next thing I know, it's 4:45 and I am still at home trying to find a new way to tie the sari so it will stay up longer than the ten minutes it takes me to jog to work.

The job at The Bagel Factory only lasted three weeks but before that I worked for six months at Café Castalano, another family-owned restaurant. I like small, family-owned places: the parents and children and cousins all work there and if they like you, they make you feel like you belong to them. In fact, the only jobs I ever apply for are at restaurants owned by families.

At Café Castalano, they grew their own tomatoes on a huge farm about six miles out of the city. They grew basil and oregano and Italian parsley in a little garden behind the restaurant and one of the their cousins was a butcher, so he cut all of their meat himself. On Sundays, a whole room was reserved for the Castalano family dinner.

The Castalano's treated me as though I was their daughter. My name is Marcie but they called me Maria and insisted I call them Mama and Papa; they kissed me on both cheeks every day when I got to work. Mama didn't speak any English but I understood her just fine. I could always tell when she was trying to get me to eat her lasagna (which looked delicious, bubbly and cheesy, with strings of fried rosemary and garlic tossed on the top) or Rosa's Gnocci, which she sometimes let me help her make. I wanted to please her, which I knew eating the specialties named for her would, but my shift at Café Castalano didn't start until 4:00—I was the evening prep cook, responsible for chopping all the vegetables and setting up all the salads—and I didn't really have time to eat. I tried to gesture to her that I was too busy to eat her food and she would nod her head: I think she understood me, too. Then she would kiss me again, hug me for a few seconds and then pat my belly, for no reason. Other than that I was pretty sure she loved me.

When I had to leave Café Castalano, I was very sorry that I had never tasted any of the specialties of the house, but I knew then and still know now that I could go eat there as a customer any time I want. I could probably go on Sunday and eat in the family's private room. I still miss Mama and her brood, especially Angela who is only thirteen, shy and awkward and chubby, and who would stand next to me at the chopping table and whisper to me about the boys she had crushes on. But Papa said that I was too slow in the kitchen. He said I got too distracted and the work wasn't getting done, though I still don't really know what he meant. I chopped every onion and tomato, green pepper and mushroom as if it was the last vegetable on earth, methodically and gently, making sure each piece was the same exact size. I never left work until I had chopped everything set out for me, so I often stayed there very late. When he told me not to come back the following morning, I asked him if that meant I had a day off: then he took my face in his hands, which were warm and smelled like basil, and he said, "Bella Maria, the restaurant work isn't good for you." I guess he was right: even though I loved the Castalanos, the restaurant work at the Café Castalano wasn't right for me: Papa must have known I wasn't meant to be in the kitchen and needed to be out among the people, like I am at The Shiva Indian Restaurant. But at the Café Castalano, you couldn't serve customers unless you were a man who spoke Italian.

I have to carry out two huge Tandoori Lamb dinners, one in each hand, the edge of the trays settled on my wrists, but I can feel the knot of my sari—which I tied so tightly—already slipping down toward my belly button. Too bad this isn't a Greek restaurant: I could do a belly dance.

A very large man with a very skinny woman calls out to me when I pass his table with the two Tandoori Lamb Platters. He recognizes them as his own and he is right but I am wafting in the mint and curry and imagining what the soft meat would feel like in my mouth so I just keep walking, I guess: I don't know where I am going; maybe to the Dancing Shiva? But then I hear my customer's voice so I immediately double-back, say I am sorry, and set the steaming dishes down. The skinny woman doesn't lift her head—she is staring at the white tablecloth—but I see the big man roll his eyes in disapproval. I ask him if he wants more bread but he just points to the large warm circle of Nan on his platter and then flicks me away with his free hand, the one that hasn't already picked up a fork.

On the way back to the kitchen, I untie and retie the sari. The restaurant is crowded, as it should be: this is fine Indian cuisine. All of the chefs and cooks are impeccably careful about their ingredients. Everything that gets chopped gets chopped into the same size pieces. All of the smells go together: coriander, saffron, lime, curry, garlic, cumin. You would be crazy to come to Miami Beach and not eat here. The Shiva Indian Restaurant is smack in the middle of Lincoln Road, where tourists flock and where locals still hang out because it isn't as crowded or pretentious as Ocean Drive. It also isn't as expensive. On Ocean Drive, you can pay $17.00 for a hamburger with American cheese; at Shiva's, you pay only $12.95 for Lamb Vindaloo. When Freddy and his wife Alexandra come here to visit me from Phoenix at Christmas, this is the first place I'm going to take them. They'll love it here, and not only because of the food: Freddy was worried because I hadn't found a job that made me happy. When he walks in, he can thank the Dancing Shiva.

Table Four is ready for dessert: this is my favorite part of the meal. At Shiva's, we have these thin silver-wrapped chocolates; they are only slightly wider than the lead from the mechanical pencils I used in geometry in junior high school. They are as light as strands of hair. You have to be very careful about tearing the silver wrapping off; when you do, you are acquainted with these thin, airy and hollow tubes of bittersweet chocolate, flavored so slightly with orange. Every third table, I peel one for myself.

Here is my logic. I come too late to eat the meal the Sahas offer to me so generously and that I crave all night long as I serve this exotic food and smell its seductive smells. When I get home, the smell is in my skin and my hair and when I try to fall asleep, I am sorry I did not eat from the hummus platter that is always out for waiters, or the pappadam, which smells so peppery and good. Because I don't have time to taste things, I toss fennel seeds into my mouth where they quiet my cravings for other mouth-watering items that threaten to make me stop in my tracks and eat the food steaming in my hands, destined for customers. It is no wonder that the seeds quiet my cravings so completely and so quickly: the Hindu god Sukra's name means seed, and he was born from the miracle-providing Shiva. Like father, like son: in seconds, I am released.

I was fired once for being too slow, and I definitely don't want that to happen again. But, still, I make time to peel three or four chocolate sticks every night because I can do it while the computer is figuring up the customer's bill. I think the cost to the Sahas is the same as it would be if I ate a meal, probably less, and I am sure the calories are less than the richer, more complicated items, given the size and airiness of these confections. As far as I am concerned, this is a plan that works for everyone.

When my arms are full of tea and chocolates and two dishes of our Green Tea Ice Cream and I am heading out of the kitchen to the dining room, I see out of the corner of my eye Mrs. Saha calling me back. She points to my belly and I think that the chocolate stick I just ate has probably already made its mark there. I feel my face burn with shame: what was I thinking? We're probably not allowed to eat those; no one has ever said we could or couldn't but I had no right to assume we could. I'm so embarrassed, I could die but it serves me right: chocolate, any size chocolate, is the most fattening food on earth: I know that. Everyone knows that. And tonight I've already had three.

Mrs. Saha comes and takes the tray from my hands and I am thinking of what I can say to apologize when I see her staring at my mid-section. I am afraid to look, afraid to see the evidence of what I have done. But I have no choice so I look down: what I see is that my sari has dropped below the rim of my underwear. Mrs. Saha makes a sound, kind of like a hum, while I pull the sari up almost to my bra and tie the tightest knot I can. When I retrieve the tray and make my way out to the dining room, I can feel it starting to slip down.

I set the desserts on Table Four and the patrons smile appreciatively. On my way back to the kitchen, I try to be discreet about pulling up the sari, knotting it again. When I get into the kitchen, the Sahas are both standing in front of the salad cooler, waiting for me. Quickly, I apologize for eating the chocolates; I explain that I didn't know they were off limits, that I promise never to eat them again, and then I confess about the fennel seeds, too.

Mr. Saha tells me it's not about the chocolates; he says I can have as many of the chocolates as I can eat and Mrs. Saha nods in agreement. It's not about the seeds, either, he says but this time Mrs. Saha does not nod; instead, she tells me she does not understand why I only eat seeds and I want to ask her what she doesn't understand since customers eat them all the time after they've finished their meals but instead I just say "Sukra." The Sahas look at each other as if they don't know who Sukra is and that's when Mr. Saha tells me it's about the sari.

At the Café Castalano, I did a bad job of prepping vegetables and I ended up slowing down the whole kitchen, though I have to say that I didn't see it that way. At The Bagel Factory, I made customers uncomfortable even though I only saw it as a difference in tastes. But here, at The Shiva Indian Restaurant, it is merely a matter of my sari: it's just that I cannot make it stay up. I suggest to Mr. Saha that maybe if I cut some of the fabric away or use safety pins that I can work this little problem out but Mr. Saha tells me that he thinks it's best if I just go home now: they will mail me the rest of my pay.

Now it is me who doesn't understand. I am a good worker at The Shiva Indian Restaurant. I get here on time, never ask to leave early (like some of the other girls do), and I am this restaurant's biggest fan. When I present the food to my customers, it is with a kind of pride as if I'd made it myself. I tell them how delicious it is (though I have never tasted any of it, I am sure from the smells), direct their attention to its textures and colors. My devotion is so complete that tonight I almost walked away with two Tandoori Lamb dinners. And I barely eat a thing, only a few seeds, so I know I am saving the Sahas some money.

Except, maybe, for the chocolates. Something so delicate, so perfect, must cost a fortune to make and to buy. I remember one time when my mother got chocolates as a gift from her boss; she never said we couldn't eat them so Freddy and I tried two or three out of every row. When she came home and saw what we had done, we didn't have time to run: for a long time after that, I couldn't eat hardly anything—and definitely nothing solid because it was really painful to open my mouth and then there was what happened to some of my teeth—so I guess after a while I just got used to not eating much and it was never really a problem until I came to Shiva. But now I am convinced that eating the chocolates must be the real reason for my being fired and the Sahas are just too kind to tell me, to embarrass me, to make me feel like a pig. I think about promising, again, that I will never pull the silver paper off a chocolate stick for myself but I can see in their eyes that they have made up their minds. And the truth is, I deserve this: the Sahas have been so good to me—they have treated me like one of their own—and all the while I was sneaking chocolate behind their backs. This time, I have to admit, the punishment—or at least this small part of it—is what I have coming to me.

Rosie

The sighing died. It was then I saw the judgment. It was the judgment of life against death. I will never see it again so forcefully presented. I will never hear it again in notes so tragically prolonged. For in the midst of protest, they forgot the violence. There, in that clearing, the crystal note of a song sparrow lifted hesitantly in the hush. And finally, one bird to another, doubtfully at first, as though some evil thing were being slowly forgotten. Till suddenly they took heart and sang from many throats joyously together as birds are known to sing. They sang because life is sweet and sunlight beautiful. They sang under the brooding shadow of the raven. In simple truth they had forgotten the raven for they were the singers of life, and not of death.

Loren Eiseley, The Judgement of Birds

The three women who worked in the flower department at the Winn-Dixie were sizing up the new girl in the bakery. Her name was Mindi and on this, her third day on the job, she was wearing a tiny white dress that barely reached her upper thigh. It had yellow flower buds all along the scooped-neck, creating the impression of a smiley face against her cleavage. Roz watched Barb, the bakery manager, frown as she handed Mindi the Winn-Dixie smock. Who *is* she trying to impress in that dress here, Roz wondered, but without much interest or enthusiasm and returned to arranging the day's bouquets. Still, Roz felt the need to try and make her fit in.

"Well, she *is* pretty, " Roz observed, tearing equal pieces of pink ribbon from the roll.

"I don't think so," Charlene quipped, "she's got a big nose."

"Oh, come on, Char," said Roz, "and hand me those daisies, will you? No, the other ones; yesterday's. I can stick them in the middle of this bouquet." Roz moved the new dyed-purple daisies apart and stuck the slightly turning white ones inside. "There," she said with satisfaction, "that's good. Besides, she has a great body; no one's going to care if her nose is big or not."

"I don't think her body is so great," Charlene said. "She looks like a Barbie doll...no one dresses like that anymore. And who wears all that jewelry to work in a grocery store, anyway?"

"Maybe they dress like that in the South," JoAnne suggested, "isn't that where she's from? The South?"

"We're from the South, for God's sake; how much more south can you get than Miami?" Charlene was tying a bandana around her hair like a headband. She had just turned twenty and could not suffer vain flirty girls like Mindi, girls who drove her out of high school before graduation with their whispering, the perpetual smiles on their faces, the rumors they spread like sacred truths and their condescension, like Mindi's, as if everything they said was at once pleasing and beneath them. The only difference was that Mindi was clearly over thirty.

"But Miami's not Southern," JoAnne pointed out, "No one drawls down here."

The store wouldn't open for another forty-five minutes so the three women were working hard to get the flower department ready. It was Mother's Day weekend; they would be swamped.

"Oh," Charlene said, "look at Jack: those birds again."

All along the Winn-Dixie sign above the store's entrance lived a community of tree swallows. Nearly every time the automatic doors flashed open, some small birds flew in. Once inside, the birds panicked and flew around like mad. They perched on the tops of canned goods displays; they got stuck in light fixtures; their droppings turned up on the glass seafood counter, in between bottles in the wine racks, once in a while in a customer's hair. Store managers had tried everything to get rid of them—even taking down the sign and rebuilding one that was supposed to be bird-proof—but nothing worked. No one knew what drew the birds to the sign but, eventually, their presence became customary. So every morning, Bo—the store's General Manager—made some stock boy chase the delicate birds down with a net and put the ones that could be caught back outside. This morning it was Jack Corcoran who was stalking two birds near the produce aisle.

"He's so funny," Charlene said. The other two looked at each other and rolled their eyes in a kind way; Char and Jack were a month or so into their own stalking ritual, something both older women remembered both wistfully and with bitterness.

"Why don't you go help him?" Roz suggested. "We can handle this."

"Shut up," Char said laughing, and went toward the cooler to get the buckets of gladiolus.

"Do you think these orchids looks good here?" JoAnne asked.

"Yeah, they do," Roz answered. "But maybe we should put the roses over here, near the pond." One of the most distinguishing characteristics about the flower department at this particular Winn-Dixe was the simulated fishpond. It was constructed at the bottom of a large plate-glass window, bordered with dark blue and green mosaic tiles and dug three feet below the floor level. A tropical fish company kept the pond stocked with standard issue goldfish, some orange and some whitish, all very fat and surprisingly fast. Roz kept a bowl of fish food on a pedestal next to the pond and let children feed the fish and squeal as the fat carp darted around the dark green pond.

"Where I lived in Pennsylvania," JoAnne had said on her first day on the job when she saw the pond, "we used to have this place on Lake Pymatuning that was called The Linesville Spillway. At the shoreline there were hundreds—I mean, hundreds—of these huge fat disgusting carp, orange ones like these, but much bigger. There was a little bridge and a stand where they sold old loaves of white bread. And people, mostly tourists camping at the State Park, would come and feed the bread to these fish. There were so many fish and they had gotten so fat on the bread that they just lay on top of each other in layers. The water barely covered them so they had to squirm around just to stay wet. All the sea birds used to walk on top of them; they make postcards with pictures and captions that say, *Linesville Spillway: Where the Ducks Walk on the Fish*. You'd throw a balled-up piece of bread in and all of these fish mouths would open and close like crazy. Then they would slide and slither on top and underneath each other to get at the bread. I used to dream about falling into those fish mouths. Ugh."

Every since she heard that story, Roz kept a closer eye on the fish, resisting the image of a small chubby child tripping, falling in, and disappearing forever in the sucking mass of greedy goldfish.

When she was done setting the roses down, however, she eyed something else she didn't want to imagine.

"Oh, shit," Roz said.

"What?" JoAnne was arranging the orchids and didn't look up.

"Let's hope Char gets stuck in the cooler. Look."

JoAnne looked up to see Mindi standing so close to Jack Corcoran, their upper arms were touching; she had one hand on his shoulder blade. When a tiny swallow swooped toward her, she let out a high-pitched squeal and moved her body in, against Jack's chest. Naturally, at that moment, Charlene emerged from the cooler.

"Fuck, " Charlene groaned, two buckets of huge gladiolus in each hand, "this is not what I need to see now. Isn't she married?"

"Doesn't seem to stop her," JoAnne said, "yesterday she spent her morning break standing next to Carlos while he bagged the groceries. Bo asked her if she knew where the break room was but she just stood there. Smiling. Then he told her where it was, and she said, 'Thank you...Bo" but didn't budge.

"What did Carlos do?" Roz wanted to know.

"Nothing. You know Carlos—he's probably in love with her by now."

"That's nothing," Charlene returned, but her eyes were beginning to fill with tears as she watched the new girl press up against the boy she thought she was beginning to love. "After work yesterday, I saw her sitting at the bus stop with Chris while he was waiting for his bus."

"What's so weird about that?" Roz asked.

"She has a car."

"Hey Rosie," Bo said, addressing all three with the one name. He had walked into the flower section, part of his morning rounds. "Has everything you ordered come in today?" Bo was quiet, about sixty and balding, steady and avuncular; everyone in the store loved him.

"I'm not sure yet," Roz said, "I still have to check the cooler. Think Jack'll catch the birds before we open?"

Bo turned to look at Jack and sighed. "Jeez," he said, "that new girl is everywhere except where she's supposed to be," and he walked toward Mindi and Jack.

Roz and JoAnne stood on either side of Charlene and watched as Bo approached them. JoAnne let out a low groan as the three watched Mindi place one hand on Bo's shoulder and then move that hand up to smooth down what was left of Bo's hair behind his ear. She still had her smiling face and impressive chest turned toward Jack. Instinctively, Roz grabbed JoAnne by the back of her Winn-Dixie smock; Bo reminded JoAnne a lot of her own father, who had died while JoAnne and her then husband Corey were driving to Miami, and she knew JoAnne's temper had no waiting period.

"Settle down, Sister," Roz said. Although they couldn't hear what Bo was saying, they could see that he was trying to be firm and they could see Mindi nodding her smiling head up and down like a jack-in-the-box. Mindi was talking then, too, her mouth opening and closing like a goldfish. She still had her wrist resting on Bo's shoulder, her hand was still touching his hair near his ear. Suddenly, Mindi began to jerk and twist: one of her many bangle bracelets had somehow gotten caught in what remained of Bo's hair. Jack, in serious discomfort, extricated Mindi's bracelet and hand from Bo's head.

"She is so fucking weird," Charlene said, "what is with her, anyway?"

"Settle down, Char: she's just a flirt," Roz offered, but she wondered how convincing she was since she felt herself wincing at the image in her head of Valene, a young silly girl Roz had also thought was just a harmless flirt until she ended up taking Roz's husband away from her, and in a single afternoon.

"She'd better stay away from Bo," JoAnne said and not kindly. "Here, you guys: help me move the rest of these orchids."

When the cooler had been checked and the flower section was in order, there was one more thing to do before breakfast. Although it was not in the flower department, the three women were also responsible for the upkeep of a large waterfall that had been constructed in the middle of the store. When they turned it on, water was swept up through the transparent cylinder in the middle and then cascaded down over various levels of fake rocks and plants. Tiny multi-colored stones were strewn on the fountain's floor along with various denominations of coins. Roz and JoAnne and Charlene pulled all the junk out of the fountain—candy-wrappers, grocery lists, chewed gum, batteries, once a tiny under-water radio—and removed some of the coins so customers could still see the mosaic pattern on the bottom.

Then they went to the bakery.

"Hi, Y'all," Mindi said. She was cupcake frosting. Fingering a huge red stone on a gold chain, the stone falling just inside her cleavage, she said, "Can I help y'all?"

Roz said. "Can I have an apple fritter?"

"Sure...Roz." As if she had read a self-help book on how to make friends, Mindi's responses nearly always included a pause and then the person's name.

"Next?"

"Blueberry muffin," Charlene said in a terse voice. She was still angry.

"You have a cute smile, Char," Mindi said, but she still hadn't moved to fill the orders.

"It's Charlene," she answered, but was unable to take her eyes off Mindi's chest. "What's with all the jewels?" Charlene asked, as if she needed an excuse to be looking down Mindi's dress.

"Oh, this?" Mindi said, in a grating sort of babytalk surprise, as if she hadn't been trying to draw their attention to it. "This is a ruby someone gave me, someone who was very special" and she cast a bizarre melodramatic look out into the grocery store as if it was an ocean horizon across which would come her special friend.

"Ruby, my ass" Charlene mumbled. "The muffin?"

"Right away." Mindi went off to get the fritter and the muffin. When she returned, JoAnne said, "I'll have a bagel."

"Sure...JoAnne." As Mindi walked away to get the bagel, JoAnne muttered, "her ass is hanging out of that dress."

Roz quieted her best friend with a pat on her shoulder. Still, her internal alarm began to sound. There was something about the way Mindi operated that practically shouted: *here I am. Look at me.* Like young housewives in advertisements from the 50s, she stood in a model's pose, with one hip swiveled out, suggestive and coy at the same time, that frozen smile, one arm bent unnaturally at the elbow, ready to display a can of Pledge. She swayed her back so that her breasts stuck up like faces aiming for the sun. Without either woman knowing what the other was thinking, Roz had an image of Valene in a too-small bright red danskin tank top and JoAnne once more saw Lynette, the woman who Corey had left her for, and Lynette's fake perky naked breasts. The one night JoAnne had come home unexpectedly from her cocktail waitressing job, she opened the door to a naked Lynette drinking iced tea straight out of the pitcher JoAnne's mother had given her as a going away present when she and Corey left Pennsylvania for Miami. The pitcher had an insignia of their town on it; the seal cracked in half when JoAnne brought the pitcher, tea and all, down on Lynette's enhanced cheek bone. Lynette was from Mississippi and when she screamed, it was with a southern drawl.

"Where are you from?" JoAnne asked Mindi, as she sashayed her way back with JoAnne's bagel.

"Me? The Bluegrass State of Kentucky"

"Um," JoAnne said, looking away from Mindi's ample

cleavage.

"Here, I'll pay for all that," Roz said, because it was her day to buy breakfast and it was clearly time to go.

"Oh, Kentucky is beautiful," Mindi said, as if someone had asked, "lots of horses and farming and big steaks. I just love a big steak: where's the best place for a big steak here?"

"The meat department," JoAnne said, imagining the one Corey had probably had to put on Lynette's eye after the pitcher episode. "Can you cut that bagel in half? Please."

"Carlos said **T-Bones** has the best steaks in Miami, JoAnne" Mindi continued, ignoring JoAnne's request and wrapping the whole bagel in a piece of tissue. "He's going to take me there, he said."

"Carlos is going to take you to dinner?" Roz said, surprised. Carlos was nearly seventy, married, a father of four and a grandfather of seven.

"Well, sure," Mindi replied, "being that I'm new to Miami and all. *You* know, JoAnne," she continued, ignoring Roz, "sometimes a girl just has to have a big ole steak."

"This is Roz, the person who asked you the question." JoAnne was nasty but Mindi was unflappable.

"Bye y'all," Mindi sang out. "Have a great day."

"Hey, Rosie." Jack was sitting next to Charlene on an empty overturned flower bucket; she had given him half of her muffin.

"Hey Jackson, how's the bird business?" JoAnne asked, and went over to give him a kiss on the cheek. "Catch anything?"

"Well, he sure tried," they heard Mindi saying and when JoAnne turned around, she saw Mindi standing behind her, "but I got so scared, didn't I? I saw that bird coming and I just screamed. I do not like birds," and she turned her smile on Jack.

Roz had been standing beside JoAnne but when Mindi walked up behind them, she automatically moved away, as if from a bad smell. As if it had been choreographed, Mindi had stepped into the space where Roz had been and moving in front of

JoAnne, she stopped exactly between her and Jack. Charlene just glared.

"Isn't the store open now?" Roz asked quickly to diffuse the tension that was building fast. "Shouldn't you be in the bakery?"

Mindi remained in her spot, smiling, but she didn't move. Roz was considering how she would stop JoAnne from clocking Mindi from behind when Jack stood up and said, "Yeah, I have to go. Thanks for the muffin, Char. See you guys later," and he went off. Then just as quickly, Mindi left too.

"What the hell was that?" JoAnne was incredulous. "How did she get here so fast?"

"Maybe she's a witch?" Roz mused.

"She's a bitch," Charlene said.

"That chick is up to something," JoAnne said.

"Do you think she likes Jack?" Charlene asked in a tone that had changed from anger to desperation. "I think she does." Despite the obstacles she'd already overcome that had made her tough and snarly and wiser than her years, Charlene was still very young when it came to romance. For this, Roz and JoAnne were grateful; they wanted for Char what they themselves had lost and both would try and protect Charlene in this area at any cost.

"She's married, honey," Roz said, "besides, Jack likes you. We all know it. Everyone knows it," and Roz bent down to give Charlene a kiss on the top of the head, a gesture that seemed to dry up whatever tears might have threatened to fall.

The store opened and all morning a steady stream of customers came through the flower department. The flower department at this particular Winn-Dixie was famous in Miami; it took up the space of a small market itself and boasted the biggest and most unusual selection in the city: and Roz, with a Masters degree in Botany and a true artistic flair, mixed and matched dramatic bouquets that could be found nowhere else. The fact that it took three full-time employees to run this one department efficiently was testimony to its popularity.

Roz and JoAnne and Charlene were very busy waiting on people, restocking flowers, tying ribbons and blowing up Mother's Day balloons. Twice, JoAnne tried to shoo tree swallows from the fake nests that housed gardenias and Charlene had to excuse herself from her customers for a minute to coax them out. Everyone ooohhed and aaahhed when the tiny swallows left the bushes to peck fish food from Charlene's palm. She had a way with the small birds.

Despite the rush of business, Roz found herself looking over at the bakery every chance she got. She had to admit that the new girl's antics this morning had left her with a sense of real discomfort. There was something more than false about her, something alien: she looked through you and nodded, but didn't hear a word you said. Her smile was mechanical, her voice unnaturally high; while she kept a physical distance when talking to the women—always looking over their heads—she stood too close to the men she encountered in the store. Every one. Any one. She was always patting an arm, resting her hand in the small of some guy's back, touching someones' hair. It wasn't the kind of behavior anyone in authority could reprimand; at best, Mindi's petting and pawing could be called inappropriate, yet to Roz it felt more dangerous than that. It seemed too close to the behavior she had ignored the day she and her husband met Valene.

Valene's car had broken down in front of their house. Roz could still see Valene standing right up against Mike as he worked on her car in the driveway. Later that morning, Mike had towed Valene's car to the repair shop he owned. On the way, they drove Roz to school. Squeezed into the truck's cab between Valene who smelled like cheap strawberry lotion and the passenger side door, Roz had withstood Valene's endless prattling about how God works in mysterious ways and so it couldn't have been just luck that she had broken down in front of a mechanic's house— and one who even owned his own shop—but Roz had just pegged Valene as an obnoxious, harmless flirt. When she got home at the end of the day, with two salmon steaks, charcoal for the grill and something very important to ask her husband, Mike and Valene were waiting for her in the living room. This is God's will, Valene had said while Mike stared at the carpet.

Wrapping an azalea bush with pink cellophane, Roz knew she agreed with JoAnne: this Mindi chick did seem to be up to something, but what it was Roz could not figure out. What could you be up to in a grocery store? Still, the phony innocence and predatory gestures raised up all of Roz's protective instincts. She would not let this girl threaten what was brewing between Charlene and Jack; she would keep JoAnne from being charged with assault.

Mindi stood at the bakery counter smiling like a mannequin. Her head moved from side to side robotically, the smile never wavering. She wore dramatic eye makeup and as much jewelry as she could fit on her wrists, ears, neck and ankles.

It's like driving past a car wreck, she said to herself: I can't stand to watch her and I can't take my eyes off her. Blessedly, the flower department was suddenly packed with customers and Roz spent the rest of the morning at the bouquet table, while JoAnne and Charlene suggested mixed plant arrangements, wrapped flowers and plants in green tissue and fat purple bows, kneeled down beside toddlers while they fed the fish.

The lunch hours in the flower department were, necessarily, scattered and JoAnne and Roz always tried to maneuver theirs so Charlene could eat with Jack. Usually, that meant Charlene went first.

"I'm starving," JoAnne said, "when is Char due back?"

"She has another half an hour," Roz answered, looking at her watch and thanking a customer as she handed her a pot of white tulips. Just then, Charlene came storming back into the flower department.

"What..." Roz started to say but Charlene cut her off.

"Don't ask. Don't even ask. Just go to the lunchroom, ok? One of you? Will you go already?" She was furious, moving back and forth rigidly in front of the pond.

"Jo, you go," Roz said, "you're starving. Go on."

When JoAnne had gone, Roz asked Charlene what was the matter, though looking over at the bakery and seeing Barb juggling four customers alone, she had a pretty good idea.

"That bitch is in there," Charlene sneered, "and you won't believe this: she brought Jack lunch."

"What?"

"Yeah, she brought him lunch. And not just a peanut butter sandwich. When I got in there, she had this stupid checkered tablecloth and plastic silverware and plastic wine glasses filled with apple juice all set up. She had all these open Tupperware containers with like fried chicken and fruit salad and some corn thing..."

"What's Jack doing?"

"Whew, I don't even know. When I got in there, she was sitting by herself, right in front of this set up, sitting straight up like a goddamned pencil, but not eating. I walked by her and said, 'you sure made yourself a fancy lunch' and she said, 'thank you, Char.' Thank you for what, I was going to say but I just went and sat down with Rudy and Todd. Then about ten minutes went by and she hadn't even touched any of that food she'd brought and then Jack came in and he started to come over to where I was sitting and she said, 'Jack? Oh, Jack? I made you a Kentucky picnic' and Jack looked freaked out and he said, 'oh, thanks, Mindi, but I brought my own lunch' and she goes, 'but don't you remember? I was telling you about my mamma's famous Kentucky picnics and here, I made you one. Your lunch will keep' and he looked at me and I shrugged my shoulders so he just walked over and sat down with her. Everybody in the lunchroom was staring at her but she acted like she and Jack were the only people there. She started taking food out and tucked a napkin in his shirt and I...oh, I just got up and walked the hell out."

Roz shook her head back and forth as if to get the image out of her mind. That girl had balls, Roz had to give her that. Three days on the job—she didn't really know anyone and Barb complained that she hadn't even bothered to learn how to position the baked goods in the cases or to run the cash register—but here she was bringing a table-clothed picnic with homemade fried chicken into the Winn-Dixie lunchroom for twenty-two year old Jack Corcoran. She was married and, obviously, older and more sophisticated than Jack: What did she want with him? But more important right now, Roz had to calm Charlene.

Just then JoAnne came back into the flower department, with her container of yogurt.

"Well," she said, tossing the half-eaten yogurt into the trash, "that ruined my appetite."

"What was Jack doing?" Charlene ran up to JoAnne and nearly knocked her over. "Sorry, Jo. What's he doing?"

"Oh, baby, I'm not sure I want to tell you this."

"You have to, or I'm going back in there to kill them both." Charlene wiped some tears away with the back of her hand as real anger started replace worry.

JoAnne sighed. "Well, she's got this checkered napkin tucked in his shirt and she's explaining all of the foods she made, 'all bah mahself.'"

"I'm puking," Charlene said, "but go on."

"Then she lifts up a chicken leg, describes it, and hands it over; then she sits there with her stupid ass smile and watches him eat."

A group of four girls who clearly worked together and were on their lunch hour came rushing into flower department for Mother's Day bouquets, so the women had to suspend the conversation. Roz never did go to lunch. By the time there was a lull, they were all standing in front of the pond, their heads partially obscured by some hanging baskets of impatiens, watching Mindi smiling at customers from behind the bakery counter.

"I'm going over there to talk to her," JoAnne said.

"And say what?" Roz asked. Although she was disturbed, she knew there really wasn't anything that could be said. Charlene and Jack hadn't formalized their relationship in any way. And even though Mindi was clearly flirting with Jack, she could fall back on the fact that all she'd done was bring him in some lunch. Roz didn't want JoAnne or Charlene to make fools of themselves. Or do anything they'd regret.

"I don't know. Maybe I'll tell her to lay off. Maybe I'll tell her to fuck off."

"Oh, let me do that part," Charlene said, facing her nemesis straight on, from behind the row of hanging plants, "let me tell her to...oh shit: look at that."

Roz and JoAnne followed Charlene's glare to the bakery counter and saw Mindi feeding a doughnut to Rudy. "What the hell...?"

Rudy was a sixteen year old boy in grade eight at a high school for developmentally slow kids. He and his family lived next to Bo and Bo had hired him two years ago to work at the store on weekends during the academic year and every day during the summer. He was incredibly sweet and very naïve; all of the Winn-Dixie employees were devoted to him, but he was especially bonded to the women in the flower department, the Rosies, who looked out for him and came to his defense when customers became impatient or were rude to him. Now the women watched as Mindi pulled the doughnut away from Rudy's mouth and wiped some powdered sugar away from his lip with her forefinger before inserting the pastry again.

"That's it," JoAnne said and she headed off to the bakery before anyone could stop her, though no one wanted to.

"*What* are you doing?" JoAnne demanded to know. "Rudy, are you on a break?"

"Yes, maam, Rosie," Rudy said shyly, his glance shooting directly to his feet.

"Well, go to the break room then, honey. Do you want to take something with you? A doughnut or something?"

"Please, maam," he said.

"Mindi," JoAnne said with authority, "give me two glazed doughnuts." Mindi smiled that infuriating smile, but did not move.

It was as if she was standing her ground: JoAnne could feel her blood pressure rising. She put her clenched fists behind her back.

"The doughnuts? You actually have to go and get them." Involuntarily, JoAnne's fists appeared on the counter.

"Two?" Mindi asked sweetly, "both the same kind?"

JoAnne leaned further over the counter, so close to Mindi's face that she could see her pores were filled with foundation: "Go get two fucking glazed doughnuts right now before I fly over this counter and put your lights out." Unfazed, Mindi backed away from JoAnne and as if she had all the time in the world, went to get the doughnuts.

When Rudy had gone, Mindi stood smiling at JoAnne.

"Rudy is a boy, a sixteen year old boy. And he's got some problems, ok? You can't be feeding him doughnuts like that. Do you understand?" JoAnne was talking softly but with a hard flat anger; at the same time, a flaring frustration threatened to make JoAnne's hands assume a life of their own and grab this little twit's neck to twist her smiling face off.

"All right, JoAnne" Mindi said, quite calmly.

"And about Jack..."

"Jack is so sweet. I made him lunch today. But I'm worried about you."

"What?" JoAnne stepped back, disarmed, "You're worried about me? What are you talking about?"

"You seem upset. Are you all right?" Mindi tilted her head and pressed her eyebrows together, a look of deep concern.

"I'm fine," JoAnne said, tight-lipped and furious. "Just fine. Happy as a clam. If you need to worry, worry about yourself: you don't even know me."

"But I'd like to get to know you better. Can we have coffee sometime?"

This threw JoAnne off guard again but only for a second. "No," she said, "no coffee."

"Oh, well, how 'bout a drink then?"

"You don't get it, do you? I didn't come over here to make friends, Mindi. Quit messing around with all the guys. Leave them alone." Just then, Chris from the meat department came up to the bakery and as soon as he did, Mindi turned her smile from JoAnne and settled it on Chris, as if JoAnne's anger and this exchange had not taken place.

"Christopher," she heard Mindi say, "I haven't seen you all day. Do you want to try the éclairs?"

*   *   *

"She called him 'Christopher'? No one calls him 'Christopher'. Christ, she's only been there three days."

"Maybe she knew him from before?" They were at Roz's having pizza and venting.

"She just moved here a week ago: she doesn't know anybody," Charlene said. "I can't deal with this, I really can't."

Although Roz and JoAnne did not want to admit it to Charlene, both women were coming to the realization that they couldn't deal with Mindi either: she reminded them too much of the ridiculous bimbos who had changed their lives forever. At the same time, she was just an obnoxious flirt, someone who seemed ridiculous to them and yet somehow threatened them at a deep but inexplicable level. Perhaps is another world, Roz and JoAnne and Charlene would have hated each other, too; but timing is everything and the way they came together—grieving, abandoned, untrusting, closed up—and the way they reset themselves together to form such a bond that everyone called them by the same name, Rosie, made even the perceived threat of someone invading their territory alarming.

*   *   *

The effort to avoid obsessing over this girl who wasn't worth her time and over this situation that wasn't even a situation required nearly all of Roz's mental energy when she was alone because it raised up images she had thought were permanently submerged. On the following Sunday morning, before work, Roz was in the small garden she tended for her landlord, pulling stubborn weeds out from around the hibiscus trees. She was troubled by her inability to separate the vapid self-absorbed Mindi from the overly made-up and Bible-thumping Valene: perhaps it was the way they both exuded a fake innocence while they pushed their cleavage into everyone's face. Roz had been working very hard for the last five years to stop thinking about Valene. With her braless breasts and born-again Christianity, her wide red-lipsticked smile and high-pitched childlike voice, and Roz's ex-husband whose child she was now carrying, Valene was all the pain Roz had once thought would never subside. Roz and Mike had been married for fourteen years: they had a house, a full garden, mango and orange and lime trees, a business they had started together that became so successful, Roz could afford not to work and to pursue her Botany studies full-time. When Mike told Roz he was in love with Valene, after the two of them had spent only one afternoon together in the shop, Roz had understood what other people meant when they said the world could crash down in an instant, without warning.

But in the last couple of years, Roz dreamt about Valene less and less; she became easier with the sleek spacey Miami girls who bought flowers from her; and thanks to JoAnne and Charlene, she was beginning to regain some trust, some joy. Somehow, the anger Mindi breeded in all three women produced a kind of tension at work that had never existed before; Roz deeply resented this intrusion, this threat to the place these three shattered women had made and kept peaceful, satisfying and good. Worse for Roz was the fact that within the last few days, Mindi's persona had resurrected the simmering anger and constant anxiety about Valene that Roz had thought she finally escaped.

The day she came home from school to find Mike and Valene waiting for her on the couch, she had been thinking about having a baby. Strange thought for her and she and Mike had not ever really discussed it, despite their many years together. But on the bus ride home that day, Roz had watched a new mom with her six month old son and she thought to herself, 'I'll get some salmon steaks, grill them up, and just mention a family to Mike. Who knows?'

Less than an hour later, she had packed a small bag and left the house whose walls she'd painted cream and olive green, whose garden she'd planted by herself, whose windows she'd bordered with curtains she sewed, whose toilets she had scrubbed. On the day she had come to get the last of her things, she had screamed at Mike, "What am I supposed to do now?" and from the bedroom, she heard Valerie say, "Pray, Rosiland. All any of us can do is pray." Mike had grabbed Roz around the waist to stop her before she got to the bedroom door. He had never raised his voice or a hand to her before, or attempted to protect her the way he was protecting Valene from her. When they struggled she fell down on the hard wood floor she had polished on her hands and knees. Struggling to get up, she knew her wrist was broken but it was her cracked heart that made crawling out of the house so hard.

Aching, Roz collected the yard debris and put it in the trash. The Winn-Dixie, oddly, had been the thing that saved her. Although hot-house flowers were a far cry from the mangroves she studied during her graduate work in botany, the job somehow made her feel useful, important. The cutting and arranging, the ordering, the smell—the beautiful smell of the flowers all day long—began to calm her rage and provided purpose. Bo left all of the ordering, displaying, sales and specials up to her. And the hiring. The night JoAnne rented the apartment below her own, Roz had met her in the trash room. The two struck an immediate bond and that night, they went out for beer and wings and each woman told the other her story. They admired each other's guts and courage; they traded fantasies of how to get back at their exes and their girlfriends: mud giving way on mountain paths just at the edges of cliffs; cars inexplicably unable to stop; gun cleaning gone wrong.

For a long while, their bond was dependent upon their shared anger. And sadness. But then they became dependent upon each other for more ordinary things, as well. Because they lived in the same building, they often ate their meals together, went to the mall, made popcorn and watched videos. They disagreed sometimes but never argued; they did each other's laundry; they went on vacation. They respected and treated each other's memories and pain. Although neither woman could see it coming, they became like a couple, like the kind of couple they had wanted to be with their husbands and now only in reconstructed memory, believed they had been before disaster struck each one. And two years ago, when Roz hired Charlene, driven out of high school by a heartless clique who had discovered she'd had an abortion and whose parents were shamed to the point of disowning her, they both ended up loving Charlene like a daughter, after they had both thought they'd hate her like an ex-husband's lover because she was small and beautiful.

By the time Roz got to work, three tree swallows were flying around the ceiling over the bakery. Bo had asked Ben from Produce to get the net. JoAnne was hauling the cart of potted philodendrons out of the cooler. It was Sunday, Mother's Day, and Roz knew there would be many last minute husbands and children relieved to find plants with bows already wrapped around them saying, "Number One Mom". She was also hoping she could sell a few of the ficus trees that bordered either side of the pond.

"Oh my God," Charlene said, running into the flower department and nearly knocking over a basket of lilies set on a fake marble pedestal.

"What?" Roz said, alarmed. "What's the matter?"

"I just saw a pair of cardinals. Male and female," she was practically out of breath.

"Jesus, Char," JoAnne was annoyed, "you scared us half to death. What's the big deal about seeing cardinals? They're everywhere."

"No, you don't understand. Cardinals are my favorite birds. When I was little, I had all these bird feeders in our yard; it was the only thing my parents would let me do besides play the piano and go to Bible Study. Every free minute I spent with the birds and two of my feeders were just for cardinals. The same pairs came back year after year," she said, I really think they came back to see me. Come, come look at these."

The Winn-Dixie had a "camping" department; it had been Bo's idea and actually it was filled with more picnic than camping items: Styrofoam coolers, hamburger and hot dog rolls, chips, marshmallows, skewers, charcoal, jars of condiments and pickles. But Bo had brought in some fake shrubbery and set up a tent and an electric lantern; he had also rented a six-foot tall stuffed bear for the seasonal display from a local theatre company that was closed during the summer. The pair of cardinals—brilliant red male and his muted grey-brown mate—were nestled in the fake bush.

"Look at that," Roz said.

"Should we go get Ben? He's got the net today," JoAnne suggested.

"Oh, let's leave them," Charlene pleaded, "look how sweet they are. They're not hurting anyone. Besides, they make it seem more real. I'm going to ask Bo."

Bo was on his way to the meat department when he saw his flower department staff clustered at the display.

"Going camping, girls?" he asked.

"Bo, look at this: live cardinals in the dead bush," JoAnne said, laughing.

"Can they stay, Bo?" Charlene asked, like a little kid who wanted to keep a stray cat.

"Sure, why not?" he answered, "they can sleep in the tent with the crow that got in here this morning."

"A crow?"

"A crow," Bo stated, "flew right in as soon as I checked

the automatic doors this morning. Don't know where he is but maybe he'll eat the swallows."

"Crows won't eat swallows, Bo." It was Rudy, and he was walking through the camping area on his way to get some breakfast at the bakery. "They're not hawks, you know."

Bo looked at Rudy and then back at the girls; he rolled his eyes and ran his hand over the top of his head as if there was hair there. "Crows aren't hawks, you know," he said, "and this from Rudy." He shook his head and went off to check on the meat.

The girls were on their way back to the flower department but they stopped when they came to Ben staring up at the tree swallows, perched on the steel molding over part of the dairy case. Where there had been three just a few minutes ago, now there were about a dozen.

"Now what?" he said to no one in particular. "There's no way I'll get them all in this net."

"Oh, leave them," Char said, "who cares. They're just birds. They're cute."

"Bo really wants me to try and get some of 'em out," Ben said, "but who knows how?"

The girls nodded their heads and started off back to work. As they rounded the bread and cracker aisle, just at the front of the store, they looked up to see several different kinds of birds flying above them into the store. As if they were one, all three looked down immediately and saw that the automatic front door seemed to be stuck in its wide open position. In the space where the doors normally met to close, Mindi and Jack were crouched down on the ground and moving their open hands all over the floor.

"What the hell?" JoAnne said, loud enough to be heard.

"My purse," Mindi said, in a kind of weepy voice that made JoAnne want to shoot her. "Me and Jack were walking in and I was telling him about my Persian cats who are so funny and I was swinging my arm to show him how they jump from my bed to my bureau when my purse flew out of my hand and opened. Can you help us find my extra contacts? They fell out of the case."

Four more tree swallows flew in low, just over Jack and Mindi's heads; one dipped down toward the large gold hoop in Mindi's ear.

Mindi screamed, crouching lower and covering her head with her arms. "Help," she squealed, and lifted herself up a tiny bit into a kind of squatting position and reached up for Jack's arm. "I hate birds!"

"He's attracted to that gold earring," Roz offered. "Maybe you should take your earrings off."

"No, I can't" Mindi shrieked, "I can't lose these."

"Why? Someone special give them to you?" JoAnne said, with undisguised sarcasm that Mindi did not pick up on.

"Yes." Just then, the bird made another dive for the earring.

"Oh, no," she cried.

Jack stood up so fast, the air beneath his knees practically knocked Mindi over. Charlene just kept on walking.

"Jack?" Mindi crooned, "can you walk me to the bakery? So these birds don't swoop down on me?"

"They're not hawks," Roz said, parroting Rudy but wishing they were and that Mindi's fears would come true. Then she shifted to practicality.

"Jack, can you come and help us move the ficus trees? Closer to the front of the department?"

"Sure," he said sheepishly, as if he had been caught doing something wrong.

When they got to the department, Charlene was trying to move one of the trees herself.

"I can get this goddamn fucking tree to move myself," she said when she saw Jack coming to help. "Go on to the bakery; have a cupcake."

"I asked Jack to help us, Charlene," Roz said, sounding

like a mother.

"What's the matter, Char?" Jack said, "what did I do?" But he knew.

"How'd you end up coming into work with her?" Charlene faced him straight on, but tilted her head toward the bakery.

"She was driving past me on LeJeune and she gave me a ride."

"What was she doing on LeJeune? She lives at the Beach; it's the opposite direction," JoAnne said, feeding the fish in the pond. She tossed in a handful of fish food and the big carp swam up to suck it down. At the same time, a small bright green bird flew out of one of the ficus trees and up into the rafter at the top of the window.

"Whoa," JoAnne said, "what's that?"

"It's a parakeet," Charlene exclaimed, "oh my God: look how green he is." All three girls and Jack stared up at the bird.

"What is going on around here," Roz asked, "it's like Hitchcock's *The Birds*."

"What?" Charlene and Jack said at the same time.

"Never mind," JoAnne said, laughing and patting Roz on the shoulder. "We're old, girlfriend. But why are all these birds coming in here?"

"Who knows," Roz said, "pretty weird."

"I think it's cool," Char said.

"Me, too," said Jack, but Charlene just turned and walked to the cooler.

"She is really mad at me, Rosie," Jack said to Roz and JoAnne. "What am I going to do?"

"It's not your fault, honey, but stay away from that Mindi, ok? She's just going to cause trouble."

"I tried not to take the ride but she was inching along side me while I walked down LeJeune and it was rush hour and all these cars behind her were honking and so I just got in."

"That's ok, Jackson," JoAnne said. "Hey, go in the cooler

and bring me the bucket of Zinnias, ok? And don't come out until you and Char have made up."

As Jack walked to the cooler, Roz and JoAnne heard a squeal; when they turned around, they saw Mindi flailing around behind the bakery counter, struggling to get into her Winn-Dixie smock.

"What's she doing, an interpretive dance?" JoAnne grunted. "God I hate that girl."

"Jo, look: she can't get her arm in the sleeve."

"Why not? Too much special jewelry from too many special people? You know, she's…wait a minute: what is she doing?"

Mindi had her right arm in the smock and was struggling to get her left one in or out, it was hard to tell. But the rest of her body was jerking in a way that made her look like she was testing out aerobic dance moves; she was hopping and then jumping, squatting down and popping up and calling out for help. Just then, a good-sized glossy black bird flew out of the smock's sleeve.

Mindi leaned against the counter, hyperventilating. Mascara and eye-liner were smudged below her eyes and her tears were causing the make-up to run in tiny black strips down her face.

"Oh my Lord, oh my Lord, oh my Lord," she kept repeating on each huge exhale. "Did you see that? That creature? I stuck my arm in my smock and…" she couldn't finish her sentence. The pocket of her smock was ripped and covered with a red smear.

"Did he peck you?" Roz asked, pointing to the pocket, thinking she'd been injured, thinking she saw blood.

Mindi stuck her hand in the pocket and pulled out a squashed jelly donut.

"You had a donut in your pocket?" JoAnne asked.

"I saved it for Rudy yesterday. It was the last one and I know he loves that kind so I was saving it for him for his afternoon break, but he never came back to the bakery."

Rudy hadn't come to the bakery because JoAnne had taken a package of oatmeal cookies from the shelf and hustled him and the cookies into the employee's lounge the minute it was time for his break.

"Well, no wonder the crow was in your smock," Charlene said, walking hand in hand up to the bakery with Jack. They had seen the whole thing. "Crows are smart: they'll find a way to get food if they want it."

"Oh, I remember camping once in upstate New York," JoAnne said to Charlene, "and we had granola and gorp in our backpacks. We went down to the stream to get water and when we came back, these crows were using their beaks to untie our packs. One had already gotten into Corey's pack and was eating his gorp." JoAnne hadn't said the word "Corey" out loud in a very long time and hearing it come from her own voice stopped her cold.

"It was only a crow, Mindi," she said with her teeth clenched, a split second vision of Lynette sobbing on her kitchen floor getting in the way of her logic. "Get over it."

"It wasn't a crow," Rudy said; he had been standing behind them, waiting to get a donut, "it's a grackle. It's a Boat-Tailed Grackle."

"What?" Roz said.

"How do you know that, Rudy?" Charlene asked.

"Cause look," he said, with complete seriousness, pointing up to the large bird perched now on the fluorescent bakery light, "he's got those greenish feathers on top of the black ones. That's how you know he's not a crow. Can I have a glazed donut, Miss Mindi?"

"Rudy," Charlene said, stepping up to him, "how do you know so much about birds?"

"I watch the Discovery Channel. And my Aunt Elizabeth got me this book with pictures of all the birds. I know all the birds," he said, without affect, taking the tissue-wrapped donut from Mindi's still shaking hand. "My Aunt Elizabeth is gonna

141

take me to the Everglades to go bird watching before school starts. We're gonna see the Osprey. And a Great Blue Heron." Just then the grackle flew off toward the flower department. "Yep," Rudy said, biting into his donut, "Boat-Tailed Grackle" and he walked away.

"Are you all right now?" Roz asked Mindi.

"Yes, thank you...Roz" Mindi said, struggling back to her old self.

"Ok then, we'd better get to work."

Just then, Bo's urgent voice came over the loud speaker system: "Attention, all stock employees: all employees from stock. Come to the meat department immediately."

Jack broke into a jog when he heard Bo's call and the girls turned to follow him.

"Jesus," JoAnne said when they arrived, "look at that."

Four adult blue jays were squawking and pecking at the cellophane-wrapped packages of chicken. Bo and Randy, the head butcher, were standing there helplessly. The birds pecked furiously, ripping the cellophane away and picking up bits of chicken with their beaks.

"Wow," Roz said, "how did they get in here?"

"Lord knows," Bo said, "but we gotta get them outta here. Now."

"I didn't know Blue Jays ate meat," Charlene said, and everyone turned to look at her.

"They do cause they're omnivores," Rudy explained; he had followed them into the meat department. "They usually eat seeds and stuff but they'll eat meat if they're hungry enough."

"Oh, they're hungry, all right," Randy said. "Should we call the police?"

"The police?" asked Bo, "for what? Go get the nets. Where's Ben?"

Everyone who had been watching the blue jays demolish packages of chicken split up to find Ben and the nets and any other kind of device they could think of to catch the birds. Bo returned to the loud speaker and called for all store employees to come to the meat department. Pronto: there were only thirty more minutes before the store opened.

"You're not going to believe this," Carolee from Produce said, running up to the assembled group, "but there are like six birds in the penny fountain. I think they're catbirds; they sound like cats."

"Catbirds?" Rudy exclaimed, and he went off toward the fountain, mimicking their calls. "Eeow? Eeow?" he was calling as he ran down the aisle.

Now there were also a lot of other bird sounds in the Winn-Dixie. The tree swallows, which had grown in number to about twenty-five, were flapping their wings madly across the ceiling. The blue jays, which had been joined by two more of their kind and a few other large black birds that could have been crows or grackles, were squawking but it sounded like screaming.

"Stop screaming, for Heaven's sake," Barb said to Mindi, who had wrapped her arms around herself and was moving her torso up and down; she looked like she was praying.

"I have to go," she said hysterically, "I hate birds." She continued rocking up and down; periodically, little shrieks would come out of her mouth when the birds flew over her head.

"Jesus," Charlene said, "There just birds; they're not going to hurt you."

"I have to go," she wailed. "I can't stay here."

"So go already," Charlene said.

"No one goes," Bo said, an unprecedented authority in his voice, "until we get rid of these birds." He looked up and could not believe that the space above his head, all throughout his grocery store, was filled with flying birds. There were too many brown tree swallows to count, but he could also see small fat electric-green birds, the parakeets. The cardinals had flown out of the fake bush and were flying overhead. Blue jays moved in and out of the chicken section, huge black birds were zinging back and forth down the aisles.

"If anyone leaves, they're fired. Now someone, Jerry, go and get me a hose. The rest of you go up and down the aisles and see what's going on. Move," he shouted and everyone did. Roz and JoAnne and Charlene wanted to make their way back to the flower department to see if birds were still planted in their ficus trees, but they cut down the snack food aisle on their way. Mindi followed closely behind.

"Don't leave me here," she pleaded, but the girls ignored her.

Barb said, "Mindi, you come to the bakery with me."

"No," she shouted, "I can't be trapped back there with those birds," and she headed into the snack aisle.

A family of grackles had their heads in the clear plastic bags of Fritos. A large one, probably female, was pecking at a smaller one: her son? When she pulled a corn chip out of the bag, he tried to take it from her beak and she dropped it and pecked him away.

"Parents," Charlene said with a disapproving laugh, as she shooed the mother away.

The snapping of birds' claws and wings against the plastic snack wraps took up the whole aisle. The Rosies moved swiftly, waving their hands to scare the birds away but as soon as they cleared one section, the birds would fly back down and resume their pecking and eating. Mindi zig-zagged down the aisle, trying to avoid the dodging birds that the other women were swishing away. She kept imagining the birds' wings were clipping her hair and she threw her hands up suddenly to shake them out, though none ever came that close to her head.

"For God's sake, pull yourself together girl," JoAnne shouted when she turned around and saw Mindi flailing down the aisle as if she were on fire.

"I can't, I can't" Mindi wailed, "I'm going to go crazy." Now her foundation was running too and she was beginning to look like the lead in a horror movie. JoAnne, who had grown up in the country, had never seen anyone react like this to something as harmless as birds. She walked over to Mindi and took her by the shoulders.

"Snap out of it, Mindi," she said with some force, "we have to work together here."

"She's worthless; get her out of here," Charlene said. "Or use her to scare the birds away."

"Char," Roz walked up behind her, "come on: give her a break. She's hysterical." Charlene looked at Roz and saw the real empathy in her eyes: "Come on, honey, she's really scared." And Charlene understood.

Together with JoAnne, the Rosies formed a circle around the shivering Mindi and pushed her gently toward the flower department, which was now full with the sound of twittering and clear bell-like singing. In unison, they set her down gently in a corner on the floor.

"The parakeets," Charlene gasped when she saw how many there were. Dozens, perched in the ficus trees, shimmying their fat emerald and yellow bodies into the fake nests that housed mixed plants, skimming the fish pond water for stray bits of food. "They look like Christmas lights," Charlene said, "when they fly, they flicker. Beautiful."

Bo's voice over the PA system cut through the birdsong; he was telling everyone to get plastic from the storeroom, to open boxes of trash bags and to cover every item in the store that was not waterproof, which was nearly every item in the store. They were going to turn on the fire system and wash the birds out. But Roz and her friends, with a simpering Mindi on the floor, were too mesmerized to move.

"It's like an aviary," Roz said, "a bird sanctuary. It's unbelievable."

"Amazing," JoAnne agreed, "I've never seen anything like it."

"I've got to get out of here," Mindi cried, but she couldn't move.

"Quiet down, Mindi," Charlene said, "I can't hear Bo or

the birds over your whining."

"Will you come with me, Char?" Mindi begged, still squatted down and covering her wet melty cheeks with her palms.

"Don't press you luck honey," Charlene said. Mindi hid her head below her open hands and groaned. When Charlene turned around to look at her, she saw something she had never realized she'd wanted to see for most of her high school years: Mindi was a mess. Her make-up was completely smeared and her nose was running; she'd put her hand through her hair so many times that it had fallen greasy and flat onto her face. Mindi looked like the beautiful girls who made fun of Charlene's clothes, the ones her mother made and forced her to wear; she looked like the girls who snipped off her hair with sewing scissors in Home Ec, who pushed her into the pool before she'd changed into her suit: Mindi looked pathetic, with all the trappings of her image melting in her tears and fear. Mindi had wrapped herself in the Winn-Dixie smock and was rocking back and forth while she sat on the floor.

"Mindi," Charlene said in the quiet voice she'd used yesterday to coax the birds out of the trees," don't worry, ok? These are birds; they aren't interested in you." Then she patted Mindi on the head and moved away.

While most of the store's employees were opening trash bags and flattening them against the shelves of paper goods, rice and pasta, bins of produce, bags of snacks—all the while flicking all sorts of birds out of their way with arms and brooms and dusters—the girls in the flower department were staring at the community of parakeets that had taken roost in their trees and plants. Rudy had gone behind the bakery counter and lifted himself two huge crème puffs. Slowly, with his eyes up in the ficus trees, he made his way into the flower department.

"See those ones with the yellow under their wings?" he said, as if he was delivering a lecture, "the ones who are real still on the light? Those are White-Winged Parakeets but I don't know why they call them that. They're not white," he observed, confident, and licking bright white crème from side of his pastry.

"What are the other ones, Rudy?" Roz asked.

"Oh, those? Those are called Monk Parakeets. They're really bright green. Those are the basic kind we have here in Florida." He sat down on the floor, biting into his crème puffs but keeping his eyes on the birds.

"Rudy?" Mindi cooed, edging herself on her butt toward the mesmerized boy. "Could you walk me to the door?"

"No, Miss Mindi," he said, "I have to watch the birds."

"But couldn't you just walk me first," she begged, "and I'll give you something."

"I don't need nothing, maam," he said.

"Another crème puff?"

"Oh, Rosie won't want me to have more than two, right Rosie?" he said, flicking his glance for a split second to the girls and then back to the birds.

"That's right, Rudy," JoAnne said, "we don't want you to get sick."

Mindi suddenly stood straight up and in a voice that no one at the Winn-Dixie had ever heard her use before, a voice that sounded as shrill as an old angry woman's, she said, "Goddamn all of you! I need to get the hell out of here right now."

"Just relax, Mindi," Roz said, looking around the store. She noticed that except for the sound of birds, it was suddenly very quiet despite all the activity that was taking place. Then she started laughing sort of quietly, out of a kind of unfamiliar giddiness, because all around them were birds in the bushes and plants and trees, and they were singing. "These birds aren't going to hurt you. Just look at them: they seem very peaceful."

"That's cause they're home," Rudy said, matter-of-factly.

"Oh," Mindi moaned, hunching over now with her legs bent and her arms wrapped around her knees.

"Home?" Charlene asked, "what do you mean?"

"It's in my book," Rudy said, folding the tissue from his crème puffs into a tiny square without looking at it, "my book on

147

native Florida birds. This is their ancient home, their roost."

Everyone turned to look at Rudy.

"Yeah," he went on, "a long time ago, like before there were buildings or anything, this was a roosting place for birds. All different kinds of birds, like the kinds in here now. And some other ones that aren't here, water ones like the Great Blue Heron 'cause there was a lot of water here, and even huge ones like the Osprey and like hawks."

"All of those birds lived here?" Roz asked, not sure if she was more bewildered by this information or by the fact that it was coming from Rudy.

"Yup. They were like a big bird family. All different kinds of birds but they all took care of each other and got food and made nests and everything. Then when man came, he started building stuff and the birds didn't know what to do. People started doing all this stuff like cutting down trees and moving the water around and lots of the birds left. Now only the ones who got used to people are still around here."

It seemed unbelievable, the story itself and the fact that Rudy was telling it. But to Roz, it all made perfect sense: she well knew how one small act of fate—a man stumbling on land fit for a building, a car breaking down on a particular street, a ditzy needy girl taking a job at a bakery—could set off a chain reaction that changed things forever. She knew how home could become a strange, terrifying place overnight, a place you had to flee, and how the longing to return never went away.

"But why did they all come in here today?" Roz asked, "how did they all know?"

"Well, I know why today," Bo said. He had just walked into the flower department and he was carrying something shiny and mangled in his hand. "Who does this belong to?" he wanted to know.

"What is that?" JoAnne asked, taking the silver thing from him. "It looks like a compact."

"Oh, it's mine," Mindi squealed, "it's my compact. It

must've fallen out of my purse. What happened to it?"

"I'll tell you what happened," Bo said, and it was clear he was, in his own quiet way, furious. "It was stuck in the bottom ridge of the automatic door; that door's been wide open since you got here, and all the birds just flew in." What Bo did not know was that after the catbirds had been spotted, Rudy had scattered bird seed all over the floor from the water fountain to the camping department to the wide open front door.

"So you're responsible for this?" Charlene said.

"Give it to me," Mindi snarled, suddenly standing up, "give that to me. Oh my God, look at it: it's ruined." She tried to open the clasp but it was crushed. "How did this happen?"

"We had to yank it out with pliers," Bob said. "We'll replace it."

"It's irreplaceable," she said. "Oh, I can't believe this is ruined."

"Ruined? You don't know the meaning of ruined," Bo said, "it's just a compact, for God's sake: you can get another one," but how will I ever replace this, he thought to himself, looking around at his bird-filled grocery store and knowing now for certain that he would have to close it down: the sprinkler system would do little more than ruin his stock and send the birds higher up for cover. Already he was wondering where Rudy could go, if Carlos—at his age—could find another job, how the Rosies would manage if they had to split up. For these last two years, without ever saying a word, Bo had watched the bond among the three women develop and solidify, three women who he had thought would hate each other and now were solid and beautiful, melted and balanced together as a sheet of unbreakable glass. This is their home, he thought, and then his gaze returned to the birds.

Charlene walked back to the ficus trees that were now full with birds. In fact, the entire store seemed inhabited by birds of all kinds, singing and cackling and flapping their wings, zipping from counter to display to counter to fake bush.

On his way to the storeroom for more plastic, Jack stopped behind Charlene and rested his chin on her shoulder to look up into the trees.

Rudy knew he had had his limit of crème puffs but he didn't think that had anything to do with chocolate chip cookies; he snuck behind the bakery counter and snitched four cookies from the tray. As he walked toward the fountain to see if the catbirds were still there, he left a tiny trail of cookie crumbs and soon a string of birds were following him.

Mindi stayed crouched in a ball behind the pedestal that held the lilies; she was still crying, and clutching her smashed silver compact, but no one remembered she was there.

Roz and JoAnne joined Charlene and Jack beneath the trees and before long, they were all holding hands. The birds had come home to roost; no matter what happened, this was the most remarkable thing that had ever happened to any of them. They were all terribly afraid to disturb it.

Valene

You expect to live forever with your husband
in a fire more durable than the world.
I suppose this wish was granted,
where we are now being both
fire and eternity

Louise Gluck, The Burning Heart

Because it was Friday night and Roz had the flu, Charlene was going to see a movie with Jack, and Peter Margolis was married, JoAnne decided right there at the traffic light that she was going to go out alone. Instead of continuing straight when the light turned at U.S.1, she turned right at Grand Avenue and headed into Coconut Grove. Why not, she thought, looking for a place to park, this is Miami: women go out on their own here all the time.

It had been over two years since JoAnne left Corey or, rather, since Corey had thought it would be all right to bring a girl home, as long as JoAnne was still at work. He hadn't planned on JoAnne finding a topless Lynette drinking iced tea right from the pitcher that JoAnne's mother had given them when she and Corey left Pennsylvania for Miami Beach. No doubt, neither he nor Lynette, who actually screamed when JoAnne came through the door, expected JoAnne to walk in, freeze in her own living room, stride into the kitchen, take the pitcher out of Lynette's hand and slam it—tea and all—into Lynette's face.

It had also been over two years since JoAnne had been in a bar, except for weekly dinners of wings and beer with Roz at their local pub. She pulled off the ballcap she wore to work and ran her fingers like a comb through her hair. JoAnne was free, still attractive, and she remembered how to walk into a bar, sit down, order a drink, drink it, and maybe have another. She took the escalator at CocoWalk up to TuTu Tango, walked in with purpose, and saw that her instincts were right: at the bar sat a woman, whose face was hidden by a mass of curly brown hair, by herself. JoAnne took the seat two down from her and felt a comraderie: urban women having an after-work drink in a hip bar.

This is as easy as I remember it, she thought, recalling the nights she'd met Corey in clubs he bragged he was going to buy when they first moved to Miami Beach. The Forge, The Living Room, The Bar Room...she'd waited in them all. They were so naïve, two rednecks who thought that escape from western Pennsylvania meant any dream anywhere else could come true. And South Beach was like a dream come true, all of the sunshine after years of grey Pennsylvania rain, the wide ocean, the incredibly beautiful people. But in a short time, everything revealed itself to be a lie, even the most basic things. Knowing she had Corey, that he would eventually come for her, made sitting by herself at these clubs quite easy; and even before Lynette, when she didn't really have him but didn't know it, the idea of faith— that he would show up and kiss her, show everyone at the bar she belonged to someone—still produced the same kind of false safety and confidence. Although it was false confidence—the fact was that once JoAnne and Corey had arrived in Miami, she'd never really had him at all—it was the only thing left from the relationship: now JoAnne positioned herself on the bar stool and thought, *what's the difference? I know how to make believe.*

"What'll it be?" the bartender said, a young girl, with short fluffy hair and fat red lips. A female bartender made it even easier.

"Scotch. Rocks," JoAnne replied, as if she drank this all the time. Which she did not. She swiveled on the stool to the right and then back to the left, scanning the room; as she did, the woman sitting at the bar said, "If you swivel too much, sometimes the seats fall off." The woman, JoAnne now saw, was actually more of a girl—maybe in her twenties—a girl whose hair had been curled with rollers. She looked to be about six months pregnant.

"Thanks for the tip," JoAnne replied. The girl nodded and shrugged at the same time, as if giving the warning about the stools was her responsibility, and took a sip of something that looked like cranberry juice. JoAnne hoped it was only cranberry juice but quickly determined that it didn't matter: she was not there to be some stranger's conscience.

Like many adults living in Miami as opposed to visiting, JoAnne and her friends usually avoided Friday nights in this part of "The Grove." It was too touristy, too expensive, too young and way too crowded. But now that she was there, she remembered how entertaining it could be to watch the after-work cocktail crowd slither in, a determined bee-line past the host and straight to one of the three bars.

The host was an attractive guy, if a bit pudgy. He was medium height and boxy; the extra weight he carried did not look bad on him but you couldn't help but notice it. He was wearing a royal blue and white tropical print shirt tucked into khakis and his hair was wet and slicked straight back; when he walked past JoAnne to seat a couple at a table, she looked up and saw that his eyes were as bright blue as the background of his shirt. She could smell his cologne, pine. Pretty handsome, JoAnne thought, in the working-class kind of way that reminded her of Pennsylvania, of home. Although she would never go back there, to that poverty and loneliness and to sweeping up hair in her cousin Ava's beauty parlor, being without Corey in Miami had made her remember with fondness the small town life they both claimed they could not wait to escape. Somehow the blue-eyed host, with his easy slow walk and good solid smile, reminded her of the less frantic pace of home.

"Ladies," he said like a statement, presumably to JoAnne, the bartender and the pregnant girl since he said it as he passed them on his way back to the host stand. No one answered, so JoAnne said out loud and more to herself than anyone else, "he seems nice" and then caught herself looking at him as he walked by. By this time, she'd had three deep sips of scotch. She couldn't actually remember the last time she'd drank scotch but but she was beginning to remember why she didn't drink it very often: it was too relaxing and threatened to mutate her into a version of the kind of predators she and Roz had sworn to hate, the kind where any man is fair game.

"Do you think he's fat?" the pregnant girl said, swiveling toward JoAnne but looking at the host.

"Me?" JoAnne asked, "are you asking me if I think he's fat?"

"Yeah," she said and when she slid herself off her stool so she could sit on the one directly next to JoAnne, JoAnne could see that although pregnant, this girl was too thin. From the front, she looked like a backwards S, head jutting out from a tiny neck, chest concave, belly extended. But she was also pretty, in an Ivory Soap Girl kind of way. The innocence of her white skin, dark curly hair and dark brown eyes might have masked her intentions if she wasn't also pregnant and hanging out at a bar. JoAnne could hear Roz's voice in her head: "this is the kind of girl who made us man-less." Their exes had dumped them for younger girls; the woman who took Roz's husband away was a teenage born-again Christian. But tonight JoAnne was hanging out at a bar and she needed a bit of help: the pregnant girl was at least a good decoy: now, neither one of them appeared to be alone.

JoAnne looked back at the host before answering the girl's question. But when she looked up from his torso to his face, she saw that he was looking straight at her.

JoAnne flinched. She took a drink of her scotch and kept her gaze in the glass. Since she had left Corey, the only man JoAnne had been with was Peter Margolis and she wasn't really with him; in fact, at the moment, he was with his wife and kids at his mother's for dinner. She looked up at the host looking at her again and felt a small ripple in her abdomen.

"No, I don't," she said to the girl, "I don't think he's fat" and she was going to add "at all" but that might have been taking it too far, since he did have the kind of girth that often accompanies middle-aged men—which he clearly was—into bar life.

"What do you think of his shirt?" the pregnant girl asked.

JoAnne watched him from the back now, as he leaned against the host podium and seemed to be looking at a reservation book. His back was good and broad.

"I think it's like a lot of shirts men wear in Miami," she responded, "it's probably the uniform here."

"No, it's not," the girl said, "it's his own shirt. By the way, I'm Valene."

"I'm JoAnne," and they shook hands. Valene's hand was bony and chilled.

"You're cold," JoAnne said. "When is your baby due?"

"Not for another five months; I'm just big already. Lu?" she called over to the bartender, "can I have another?"

"Pace yourself Valenita," the bartender said, "you want this one plain?"

"Never. Just put a little vodka in then, ok?"

JoAnne finished her drink and touched the glass of ice with her finger to show Lu she'd have another; that first one went down fast and JoAnne welcomed an old feeling of nervous excitement. A fantasy of going shopping for bold tropical shirts passed over her brain.

"So, JoAnne," Valene said, as if they had been interrupted from an involved conversation, "do you think it's um...um...'common' to work in a restaurant. I mean, if you don't own it yourself?"

Am I being interviewed here, JoAnne wondered. This girl was sort of nervy, or maybe she was drunk. But what the hell: JoAnne was having a second drink and as long as she kept on in this conversation, when she faced Valene it put her in a position to face the host so she could watch him, see if he really was looking at her.

"I hope not," JoAnne said, with a little laugh, "since I work at a grocery store and that seems a notch down from a restaurant."

"Yeah, but you're older. That's different."

Older than whom? Different than what? She hadn't had enough scotch yet to ask for clarification on these items and knew she didn't really want to know so instead she said, "do you work, Valene?"

"I'm a student," she said with what JoAnne detected as some pride, but even though she was young, it was clear that if she was a student, she had returned to school. Now that JoAnne saw her face at close range, she guessed Valene's age at around twenty-four or twenty-five.

"Oh? What are you studying?"

"Well, I haven't started yet but after the baby's born, I'm going to go to Miami-Dade Community College: I've been accepted. I'm going to study computers."

"I take classes there," JoAnne replied. "Creative Writing."

"Oh! That's so exciting. What do you write?"

Poetry of great promise, she almost said, parroting what Peter had told her early on in the term, when he asked her to stay after class. Then he had coaxed her into coffee, later that week into bed. The next day at work, in the flower department at the Winn-Dixie, her boss and best friend Roz, who lived in the apartment above hers, admonished her about getting involved with a married guy.

"Remember who we are, Jo?" Roz had said, "two ex-wives who got ex-ed because of younger women? You don't want to become the enemy."

"But I think I'm older than Peter," JoAnne had answered.

"Oh, and that makes it better?" JoAnne knew Roz was right but she was still so angry and hurt over Corey that she didn't care. Testimony to how much she didn't care was painfully evident: Peter was short and scrawny, a frustrated unpublished poet who garnered his self-confidence from the lost would-be poets who signed up for his class and thought he would take them to literary stardom. Even though their sex was too fast and surrounded by the smell of other people's trysts in the vile little motel around the corner from campus, JoAnne took something imperative away from the clear fact that this man wanted her enough to risk his otherwise stable life. After, they stayed naked in the bed while Peter made fun of the other students in the class: he called Sue Simpson's poems, *I looked at nature and was so sad* and complained that Leon Curry wouldn't revise because he thought he knew more than Peter, who continually boasted his Masters degree in English from Salisbury State in Connecticut. JoAnne would nod as if she understood but the whole time she would be wondering if Peter had chosen someone else to sleep with, would he be describing her poems as *my husband cheated on me and I'm so mad.*

Still, JoAnne never felt the need to apologize to herself for sleeping with Peter. The justification lay in her need to know how a woman could be intimate with someone else's husband; she needed this experience first-hand. Besides, Peter's wife kept him on a tight leash: they'd had coffee about half a dozen times but they'd only slept together twice. Peter's wife would never have to go near where JoAnne had been.

"I write poems," JoAnne said to Valene.

"Why kind? Rhyming?" Valene asked. She was sucking up a sip of her drink but her eyes were fixed on JoAnne's.

"Not usually. They're sad poems, though. And I'm thinking about trying to write a short story."

"I'd love to write a story," Valene said, "I used to write poetry in high school."

You and the rest of the world, JoAnne thought but did not say it. She looked down at her second drink and reminded herself to go slow. She wasn't ready to leave yet but she knew that the third drink would be her limit. In order to look over at the host and see what he was doing, how his butt looked in the khakis, she glanced up again at Valene. She was looking tired, maybe from the pregnancy or from the drinks—but her face was smooth and obviously her own. It had been hard for JoAnne to tell Lynette's age, given the amount of reconstructive surgery that girl had had; at least Roz knew Mike had left her for a nineteen year old, though why it was better to know that, JoAnne was now not sure.

"Yeah, I wrote poetry in high school, too," she said and she was about to change the subject, to ask Valene if she was waiting for someone, when she saw out of the corner of her eye, the host leading a big party—a family—to a table near the bar.

He walked by them but JoAnne did not know if he looked her way since she kept her head down.

"Do you think he's cute?" Valene asked.

"Who?" JoAnne asked, too quickly.

"The host. Mike," said Valene, and she tipped her head backwards since he had just passed them.

"Sure." JoAnne didn't want to take any chances.

"I mean really cute. Or do you think he's fat?"

"Didn't you already ask me that?" JoAnne said, wondering where all these questions were coming from. "Why?"

"I'm just wondering," Valene said, then she said, "when I have this baby and do two years at Miami Dade, I'm going to go to University of Miami and get my degree. Then I'll get a job for one of those big software companies. That's where the money is, you know."

JoAnne nodded but she really wanted to burst out laughing. Who did these girls think they were? Here was this Valene, drinking vodka in juice at a bar, four months pregnant, wondering if the host was too fat and she thought she was going to....

Just then JoAnne had a revelation that jolted her upright in her seat.

"Hey, are you ok?" Valene asked.

"Fine," JoAnne responded flatly, recognizing what was actually taking place here at the bar at TuTu Tango: Valene was interested in the host. Mike. Of course. No wonder she asked JoAnne all of these questions: she wanted confirmation that her target was worth pursuing. Although she couldn't explain how she knew, JoAnne was suddenly certain that Valene had gotten knocked up, was single, and hanging out at the bar looking for a father for her child. And not just any bar: TuTu Tango was very trendy, the drinks were expensive, and it appealed to rich tourists and local yuppies. But in the meantime, until one of them came in alone, Valene would lower herself to consider the middle-aged host with the palm-tree shirt and big gut. If Roz had been there she would have said, "I told you so." That's how these girls were: they went after what they could get to make their lives easier. No grocery store job for Valene, mother-to-be. She was going to find someone to finance her computer career. This girl knows exactly what she's doing, JoAnne thought as she pulled a twenty dollar bill from her wallet: she's got this guy in her viewer and she's about to shoot.

"Wait. Stay for one more," Valene urged when she saw JoAnne chug the rest of her scotch and begin to stand up.

"No, I can't" JoAnne said, with more anger than she wanted to release. What an idiot I am, she thought to herself, putting the twenty on the bar. What the hell is wrong with me? I'm no match for this girl; that guy'll choose her, even if she is pregnant and drunk. JoAnne stood up. "Can I have my bill, please?" she nearly shouted to Lu, who was filling up glasses of coke for a waiter at the other end of the bar. Lu nodded without turning to look at JoAnne and continued to fill the cokes while JoAnne felt her face turn warm with shame. Feeling brave and strappy having come by herself for a drink had backfired: the whole time she thought the host "Mike" was looking at her, he was really looking at Valene with her mass of black hair, unwrinkled face and thin arms hanging out of her sleeveless top.

"I'm gonna buy you one more drink," Valene said, with a confidence that made JoAnne want to smack her. "Just sit down a minute."

"Look," JoAnne said, turning to Valene but once again locking into Mike the host's blue-eyed stare, "I really have to go."

"No, stay. Please?" Valene looked as though she was

about to cry. "Just have one more drink, ok? I need to ask you something."

Lu came over to take JoAnne's twenty dollar bill which she had just lifted up but Valene put her hand on top of JoAnne's hand and lowered it and the money down to the brass bar surface. Then she lifted a finger and pointed to JoAnne's empty glass. "One more," she said, "on us."

"On us?" JoAnne asked. Who's us? You and your unborn baby?

"Yeah. On me and Mike" and she looked over at the host who was now on the phone.

"Oh." JoAnne sat down. On us, on me and Mike. So they were already together. "You guys together?" JoAnne asked, now very impatient for her third drink.

"Yeah, we're married" Valene said, sounding very much like a dispossessed teenager.

"For how long?"

"Five years," she said. "He wasn't so fat when we got married."

"Why are you so obsessed with his weight?" JoAnne suddenly wanted to know. "He's your husband; you guys are having a baby. Who cares?"

"Oh, I'm not obsessed: I'm just wondering, that's all."

But wondering what?

"He didn't work here when I first met him," Valene said, "he had his own business."

Ha, serves you right, JoAnne thought. Golddigger. "What kind of business?" she asked, happy now to be drinking expensive scotch bought by a twenty-something who thought she was hooking a ticket to the big life with a middle-aged guy who probably left his wife for this twit, and thinking she might just let them buy her another.

"A garage. He's a mechanic. That's how I met him: he fixed my car. It broke down right in front of his house. Act of God."

JoAnne lifted her head up as if she had just heard a fire alarm. Without pretense, she looked over at the host and then back to the drunk pregnant girl who had befriended her. Valene was an unusual name and JoAnne should have recognized it right away, but she didn't. In fact, it wasn't until Valene said the exact words that JoAnne had heard so many times before, that she realized who she had been talking to, and who she had been staring at.

Mike was not at all the way Roz had described him but then again, by the time JoAnne had met Roz, Roz despised her ex-husband. Roz had never talked about the clean cut of Mike's face, the big shoulders, the remarkable blue color of his eyes. JoAnne had pictured him two distinct ways: as wimpy, thin and puppy-dog like, stooped over and balding because although Roz never said what Mike looked like, she said that he could barely look at her when he said he wanted a divorce, that she had pushed him over a chair on her way out of the house they had built together; JoAnne also thought of Mike as a bully, because Roz had told her that when she went back to the house the last time to get the rest of her things, Valene had told her to pray and when Roz stormed toward the bedroom to do who knew what to the girl who wrecked her life, Mike had actually tackled Roz to the ground and her wrist had broken. This man who JoAnne had been staring at all night, who made her feel like a teenager at a dance, fit neither of those images.

Valene was still talking.

"We had to close the repair shop because there were too many bills...I like to shop and Mike's divorced so he has to pay alimony. And then I had a miscarriage and there were a lot more bills, you know? So he took this job here and now we have insurance. I can't work because I'm pregnant and all so I hang out here most nights while he's working because I don't like to be by myself too much."

"Aren't you worried about what alcohol might do to your baby?" JoAnne asked, her mind racing, wondering just what Roz would and wouldn't want to know about this situation.

"Oh, no," Valene said, "I know she'll be all right" and she patted her stomach.

"You know it's a girl?"

"Well, we haven't had the test but I know."

"How can you be so sure?" JoAnne asked, again looking over at Mike looking at her. JoAnne wondered if he had any idea who she was. Roz and Mike barely spoke to each other anymore but once in a while he called to see how things were going. At first, Roz just hung up on him. But after a couple of years, she half-participated in the surprising and infrequent conversations though she was never sure why. Once he told her he had been in the Winn-Dixie and had seen her in the flower department, arranging tulips for an Easter display and laughing her head off. That observation had enabled JoAnne and Roz to figure out exactly when he had been in because the hour they had spent trying to tie together the enormous white and red and pink and lavender hybrid tulips that kept tipping out of the vases and ribbons had been hilarious. It was Easter weekend; Roz and Mike had been married on an Easter weekend. Before he hung up the phone, Mike had told Roz he thought she looked beautiful.

"I'm sure because of Him," Valene said, looking up at the ceiling, continuing the conversation as if she was having it with herself.

"Him? Who? The father?" and JoAnne meant Mike.

"Yes, the Father. The Heavenly Father," Valene said. "He let me know my baby would be a healthy little girl."

"Great" JoAnne thought and then realized the sarcasm in her head had actually become sound in the air; she also remembered that among other things, the woman who took Roz's husband was a born-again Christian, who believed that her breaking up Roz's marriage was an act of God.

"Yes, God is Great," Valene responded. "Will you have one more drink?"

"No, hon, I've got to go now," JoAnne said and she was

already standing up.

"Are you married?" Valene asked.

"No, I'm not." But the man I sleep with is, JoAnne thought. And what's the difference? Valene wanted Mike and she took him but what JoAnne was doing with Peter, although she let him take her but never wanted him, was the same sort of crime. It didn't matter that she and Peter had an understanding, that his wife did not have to worry that her husband was going to leave her for another woman, at least not this woman. JoAnne had had sex with someone else's husband and looking at Valene, all skin and bones, swollen belly and stupid smile, all she could see was Roz: Roz gritting her teeth when she talked about Mike; Roz wondering if Valene and Mike had sex at the garage before they decided to tell Roz her life was over; Roz mixing flowers on Christmas, Easter, Valentines' Day as if the blooms would perish before she got them in water; Roz never understanding how a marriage she thought was solid and good and getting ready for the next step—a family—could dissolve in an afternoon. JoAnne was in an affair that meant nothing to her yet how was it any different? Did she really understand any better what Corey had done to her by doing the same thing? JoAnne smoothed down her shirt, took a big breath and congratulated herself: she would abandon the affair with Peter before any more damage was done. There would be some justice in this night after all.

"Why aren't you married?" Valene asked, as if being unmarried was the most unnatural thing in the world.

"I'm not interested in being married," JoAnne said and looking at Valene made it all the more true.

"Sure you are," Valene said, "you should be. Someone like you."

Someone like me.

"You don't exactly know me," JoAnne said, thinking how close she might have come to being just like this girl who had destroyed her best friend's life. She slid out between the two barstools and stood behind Mike Cardman's pregnant wife.

"But I feel like I do," Valene said.

Why, JoAnne wanted to ask but then she thought she knew: JoAnne and Roz were so much alike and now, it was clear, Mike still talked about his ex-wife. Instead, she said, "Right. Well, you take care, dear," and patting Valene on her bony shoulder, she finished with "Good bye."

"JoAnne? You know, everything's going to be all right for you," Valene called out after her.

"For me?"

"Yeah, for you" Valene said and now her voice was high pitched, urgent, as if she had to make a claim before JoAnne got away. "Everything will be fine for you, I know, as long as you do one thing."

"What's that?" JoAnne asked, turning her face back toward Valene but still moving away.

"Pray."

JoAnne turned away for good then and walked toward the door. She found the smile forming on her own face inexplicable.

She had to pass the host stand to leave TuTu Tango and as she approached, she saw that Mike was watching her.

"How was everything?" he said, as if she had been a customer who'd had dinner.

"Fine," she said, in kind.

"Thank you very much for coming," Mike said in a perfect host's voice, one that belied everything JoAnne knew about him, the things that Roz had ultimately been able to bring herself to tell: his passion for camping and fishing, the way he screamed at football players who scored or didn't on Sunday afternoons in the Fall, his skills with cars, his love for cats, his famous blue cheese burgers on the grill, the way he could do a backflip off the dock of his parents' cabin into Lake Michigan.

JoAnne stopped directly in front of him and looked into what she now realized, up close, were tired and bloodshot blue eyes. She stood there for a few seconds because she wanted a good look at the man who had given her the gift of her best friend.

"Is there something else?" he asked

"Yes," JoAnne said, feeling she ought to give back a gift in return, "Pray," and she walked out of the door.

Alta

What do women want? None of us can speak for all women, or for more than one woman, really, but we can hazard a mad guess that a desire for emotional parity is widespread and profound. It doesn't go away, although it often hibernates under duress, and it may be perverted by the restrictions of habitat or culture into something that looks like its opposite. The impulse for liberty is congenital. It is the ultimate manifestation of selfishness, which is why we can count on its endurance.

Natalie Angier, Women: An Intimate Geography

Claire needed to be sure the children were still asleep. On his stomach, seven-year-old Evan was sprawled open, arms and legs extended like a sapling. A snap of air caught in her throat as she recalled him yesterday in that same shape, flying off the high dive. Before he hit the water with a hard smack—arms, legs, belly, face, all flat as a plane of wood—she was out of her chair. But he surfaced with his curly hair wet-matted over his face, so long it covered his mouth, and she could hear his tiny maniacal giggles.

In the next room the girl, Eva, had curled her long brown body up like a bean sprouting. She could sleep through anything, this Eva, Claire's husband's child, who too long ago had lost the qualities that make children sweet and forgivable. Eva was surly and lazy, negative and unappreciative: the beach was too hot, the bike ride was too long, chlorine in the swimming pool smelled, the chicken was burnt. She didn't like to bathe, brush her teeth or use deodorant; several notes had come from school complaining of her smell.

Claire had known Eva since she was two years old, since the time she met both children's father, got swept up into his smooth beautiful arms. While Claire stood there, Eva shifted a bit in her sleep, curling tighter, clasping her hands together under her neck. She looked like a carving, her long legs bent at an angle, her already full breasts propped up under the t-shirt she slept in. At 12 years old, Eva was nearly six feet tall and every inch of her was stunning. Claire sighed as she closed Eva's door: what would this child look like at sixteen? Claire hoped she would not know. At the end of the school year, she planned to send Eva back to Haiti.

It was 8:00 am in Miami, 7:00 am in Haiti and certain the children were in deep sleep, Claire went to the phone. At 45, Georges lived in a house with seven other people. He was a talented but unlucky musician who stayed out late and woke up late and had pleaded with Claire not to leave Haiti; but he relented, even became passive, when she agreed to take Eva, too. The quickness with which he shifted from fury to détente should have been a red flag for Claire, but at that time, she was too broken to see even the most obvious signs. Now Georges was furious that she planned to send Eva back. He had bullied her into arranging tickets for him to come to Miami that evening. He was coming, he said, to have a discussion.

But Georges did not understand the word discussion. He would get off the plane with a battle raging in his head, one in which he led both armies; without even saying hello, he would start blaming Claire for not being able to love Eva, his own child who he barely knew. Evan will suffer without his sister there, he'd swear and scream. He would cry. And then he would pull Claire close and rub that soft part on the back of her neck, just below her hair. He would kiss her ear, the side of her face, her cheek and when his mouth finally found her lips, he would close in on her.

If Claire understood anything, it was her own weakness. That was why she wanted to call Georges early; at 7:00 am, he would be in a rum-soaked sleep and she would be able to disarm him. By the time he shook off enough sleep to process what she had said—that she didn't want him to come and had cancelled his tickets—the deed would be done. Since Georges had no money, the only way he could call her was collect and once she had said her piece and hung up the phone, it would be easy not to pick it back up. Claire would keep Eva for the rest of the school year, two more months: in mid-June, she would send her back home.

In her head, it sounded easy. Claire picked up the phone. As soon as it began to ring, she heard the frustratingly familiar static that was part of any kind of communication in Haiti. Then the one voice Claire hoped to avoid.

The argumentative "Yeah," a reluctant surrender.

"Can I speak to Georges?"

"Who?"

"Georges." Claire stiffened, felt her nerves thinning.

"Georges?" Gigi was playing.

Claire was not in the mood. "Yes, Georges. Can I speak with him?"

"Georges's not here."

The connection was bad, full of abrupt crackling and minute spaces of no sound at all, so perhaps Claire had misunderstood her. "What?"

"Georges's not here. Who's this?"

"It's Claire, Gigi."

"Who?"

She was about to shout out her name, to ram her existence through the weak phone lines and bloody Gigi's ear. But then she remembered the sleeping children; she did not want them to hear this conversation. "It's Claire," she hissed.

"Claire who?"

Claire who. How many Claire's were there? For Gigi, only one: the white woman married to Georges. The mother of Georges' child. The woman who made Georges regret he'd ever taken Gigi in his arms.

"It's Claire, Gigi. I need to talk to Georges."

"Georges's not here. He's at Alta's."

"Where?"

"At *Alta's*," Gigi said, exasperated, as if Claire should know what that meant. "Georges's at Alta's."

Then Gigi hung up.

Claire kept the phone to her ear, as if waiting for an

explanation but hearing now only dial tone. Alta. Gigi said "Georges's at Alta's" in the same way she might have said, "Georges's in the bathroom" or "Georges's at his mother's." She said it wearily, as if she was explaining the most natural thing in the world to the slowest person on earth.

Claire set the phone down into its cradle but did not move. In the way a fever creeps in, all of her instincts gathered together into a cold, heavy place in her chest. And as if an illness had overtaken her, Claire lied down and pulled the comforter up to her chin.

Tears could come now but Claire did not want to cry. She wanted to want to celebrate. She'd suspected it all along and now she had proof: Georges was cheating on her. With Alta. Claire searched for the justice she believed she deserved: he was a cheater, after all she had done. That was why he didn't want Eva to return to Haiti. He was afraid she would tell Claire about Alta. Georges understood, deeply, that Alta was the last thing, the very last thing, Claire could stand. He would never see her or Evan again; for him, everything would change. No more airline tickets to the States. No more summer "family" vacations to Europe or South America. No more money for his struggling band, his mother's rent, his new drums. Georges knew that after what had finally happened to make Claire flee Haiti, she would never return; but as long as he was there and she was in Miami with his children, he could live both lives. But if Claire found out that Georges was cheating, that once again he had lied, everything he depended upon would disappear. He couldn't take any chances and now Claire understood it all: he didn't want Eva because he wanted Alta.

Claire's bedroom door creaked open and Evan stood there yawning. He looked like his father—cinnamon skin, big dark eyes, mass of unruly curly hair to his shoulders. He was wearing only underpants. Claire threw the covers off and sat up so quickly, she was dizzy.

"Good morning, little man," she said, weakly, putting

her feet on the carpet to steady herself. "Come sit here with Mamma while you wake up."

Although he had gotten out of bed and come to his mother's room, Evan was still caught in the warm dreamy place of sleep.

"Can we go swimming?" Evan asked, crawling into his mother's lap and closing his eyes. She felt his head against her breastbone, wondered if Georges was kissing Alta, wondered if Alta had long or short hair, straightened or kinky.

"Sure, sweetheart," Claire said, "we can go swimming. We can do whatever we want now. You just rest."

Evan was struggling out of his dreams. "Can Eva come?"

"Come where, honey?"

"Swimming," he said, pushing himself against her chest, his head now tucked right under her chin. Eva had not come swimming yesterday; she hated the pool and wanted to stay inside and read.

"No. She cannot."

"Why not?" Evan asked; he was midway through a yawn and a stretch.

"Because Eva is going back to Haiti today."

It had come out of her mouth before she had a chance to stop it, before she knew she had decided it.

But Evan's reaction was even more startling: without warning, he jerked his head up, knocking Claire in the chin so hard that it forced her teeth together with her tongue between them.

"Damn you," she said, pushing him harder than she should have onto to the bed. "Don't you *ever* do that again, Evan, *ever*. That hurt me."

Not fully awake and rubbing both of his eyes with his small fists, Evan wailed. "You can't send Eva away. You can't."

"I can and I will" Claire said, incredulously, as if she was setting her will against an adult. Against Georges.

"I hate you," Evan shrieked, and he ran out of the room.

"Your father is at Alta's," Claire said out loud, "and you hate *me*?" She rubbed her jaw and shook her head back and forth, as if to put back together whatever the blow had dislodged. She swallowed a small pool of blood that was collecting in her mouth. The only way that Georges would be at a woman's house at seven o'clock in the morning is if he had spent the night there. She knew his habits. Her mouth throbbed. She slammed her eyes shut but the tears came anyway.

Although she wanted to crawl back under the covers and let herself cry, Claire easily gave into her regret. Feeling her way out of her room, she went to console her son. She thought he'd be in front of the television, his favorite place to pout, but the living room was empty. He wasn't in his bedroom, either. When she pushed open Eva's door, Claire found him curled up beside his sister; he'd fallen back asleep. She took the blanket scrunched up at the bottom of the bed and covered them both. It smelled of must and urine. Maybe Evan would wake and think he just had a bad dream. Maybe they both would.

Claire's tongue was pounding and she could taste the blood. She went to the kitchen to make coffee; while it perked, she rinsed her mouth with warm water mixed with salt. When Georges woke up, warm and supple from a heavy sleep, still smelling of sweat and dark rum, would Alta make coffee? Alta was dark as coffee, tantalizing. Claire had spent enough nights at the club where Georges's band played to know Alta's type intimately. She was the kind of island girl who could take anyone's breath away, dancing in front of him in a short filmy dress, more like a slip. It was bright—yellow, electric, flame orange—a drama against her dark skin: she was a flower that only blooms at night. It was the kind of tiny dress that would stick to her sweat. She glistened. He would see the outline of her breasts, breasts that had not yet fallen from age or children, the angle of her hips. He would be singing but thinking about what the flatness of her belly would feel like against his chin. He would imagine her tight slender arms around his waist and he would point his singing toward her. Alta had a wide mouth, good teeth; she wore gold chains studded with fake bright jewels, big shiny earrings. Young girls fell in love with Georges all the time and when Claire would notice, he would tell her he was just playing to the crowd. Most times, Claire could believe him. But every once in a while, there would be an Alta and Claire could see her husband strumming his guitar as if the strings were the long taut legs warming up to wrap themselves around him.

The hot coffee burned and so replaced the pain in Claire's mouth. Claire didn't wear make up; she didn't adorn herself and she dressed in modest skirts and tops. Claire didn't dance. Yet, hadn't Georges picked her out of the crowd the first time she went to the club? Every time she looked up at the band, she saw him staring at her: she had never seen a man so beautiful. When she saw him looking at her, she immediately looked away and said something mundane to Candace, her old college roommate who she was visiting and who had been living in Haiti for the six years since they had graduated. Claire had been spending those years with a Masters degree in Journalism and a significant source of money from an inheritance but hadn't figured out what to do with either: she didn't need to work so she didn't; instead, she read huge classic novels, took cooking classes and ate the results. Candace had talked her into coming to Haiti.

" While you're waiting around trying to figure it out, come here."

Claire protested, saying she could hardly take a vacation when she didn't even have a job, but then Candace said, "Haiti is not a vacation. You have time and you have money: you could be of some use here."

She decided to visit Candace for three weeks. Within two days, she knew she had never known such heat, seen such poverty or such beauty, or felt such warmth or purpose. All of Candace's friends—Haitian, American, French, Latin—embraced her and accepted her as if she was a long lost sister. She spent whole evenings with stranger's children in her lap and through them, she discovered she could sing: they called her Auntie Clar-Clar. She taught two women how to paint and sent to the States for supplies. Sometimes for dinner, she ate only mangoes. By the third day, she was volunteering at a local artisan's shop; at the end of the first week, she met two journalists, one of whom asked her to collaborate on a story about Haitian artists.

Everything in Haiti was intense: the heat, the colors of the sea and sky, the unconditional joy she felt every time anyone kissed her on both cheeks in greeting. Everything was foreign and slightly dangerous, yet Claire found a new ease within herself. All her life, she had been a loner, a person who could spend entire weekends at home reading fat novels, cooking stews, experimenting with water colors or calligraphy. Sometimes, she would stay home from Friday afternoon until Monday morning, without ever changing out of sweatpants and a t-shirt; on Monday mornings, when she forced herself to go out and look for a job, all she thought about was getting home, putting on her old sweats, and finishing her book. But in Haiti, she spent the early mornings bringing milk from a cooler to the beggar children on Candace's corner; she worked in the craft shop and then helped Candace's neighbor build his fence or read stories to children at the local school; twice, she accompanied Candace's friend Mike on his assignments for **The New York Times**. In the evenings, she went to Voodoo ceremonies and believed; she ate meats she never learned the names of; she hiked high up into hills until she thought her bones would break from the pain that made her happy, proud.

But what made her most proud during those three weeks was a small article on Haitian politics that Mike had encouraged her to write and send to **The Houston Chronicle**. It was thrilling and unreal to stand next to soldiers who were ready at any moment to open fire and then to transform their broken English into the journalism she had studied; she drank an entire bottle of champagne herself when she heard the newspaper was going to print her story.

Claire's last night in Haiti came quickly. Candace had insisted they go to a club. Claire had wanted to go to sleep early so she could take a last early morning hike, stop in and visit the strangers who had become like family, eat a bowl of cold cornmeal for breakfast. But Candace insisted.

During the band's second set, Georges never took his eyes off Claire. He was singing to her, his voice was rich and cool. Every time Claire looked up, this man with dreadlocks and beaded necklaces over his open shirt was staring through her. When she gave in and locked stares, she found she couldn't look away. What would it be like to be kissed, touched, by such an extraordinary man? She was trapped and although she didn't understand it, she recognized a familiar paralysis. Despite the confidence her experiences in Haiti had given her, when it came to men she could not deny who she knew she was: an overweight, insecure, rich white girl without a plan.

"You one lucky girl," the woman next to her said, and she nudged Claire with her hip. "The Georges want you: you must be special" and the woman looked up at the guitar player and then back at Claire. "All the girls want to be the girl Georges want," she said, and kissed Claire on each cheek.

Claire had never been the girl anyone wanted. Tomorrow, she would be back in Ann Arbor. The man called Georges was smiling at her while he sang. He knew something. Claire was beginning to know something, too: she had nothing to loose. She could fall into his seduction because she was leaving tomorrow and would never return. He probably didn't speak English: she would not even have to talk. So she smiled back, closed her eyes when his music swept through her like warm wind, licked her lips when she saw him lick his. She held herself around her hips and rocked provocatively to this music and to this man. It was the last night of her vacation and she knew she would go home to the life she left and never have any experience like the one she was on the verge of again.

That night, in his bed, she didn't know who she had

been before. In the morning, she called her mother to say she would be staying in Haiti.

Claire took her coffee to the balcony. She sipped and watched early morning boaters move out into the Bay. The commitment to leave Haiti once and for all, to raise Evan in the States, had, ultimately, been an easy one to make; in the end, it had nothing to do with the country at all. Claire lived in Haiti for eight years; in many ways, she felt more Haitian than American. She had closer friends in Haiti than she'd ever had anywhere before; and she had real relationships with the people in her community, with grocers, clothes-makers, craftsmen, artists, children, vendors, people without homes. She had bought the club Georges and his band played in and felt roots in ways that had eluded her privileged life before. Her journalism career had taken off during the Coup; by the time she left Haiti, Claire had been commissioned by a variety of newspapers and television shows all over the U.S. to cover stories, write articles, interview significant political figures. She became fluent in Creole. She had her own family now. When Evan was born, she and Georges married; soon after, she assumed care of the troubled Eva. Claire was fiercely dedicated to them all. So when it came time to think about leaving Haiti, when the violence and danger shifted the balance from her own adventure to her small son's future, the conflict set in: she needed to be there and was needed there, but she also lived with a mother's fear. Evan was nearly old enough to start school and Claire knew the kind of life her privilege could provide her young son. But there was something more sinister that haunted her thinking.

Somehow, Claire had survived all the life-threatening terrors—the shootings, car bombings, gang raids—she had encountered, not only as a journalist often in the middle of dangerous situations but also as a person living in a violent unpredictable country, a rich white person who most people either knew or knew of. But she didn't know if her luck would hold out; and while she did not want to take her son from his homeland, she also did not want to subject him to the events that had made her fearful and in some stupid ways, fearless. But most important, Claire could not bring herself to imagine what would happen to Evan in Haiti if anything ever happened to her. She had certainly seen what had happened to Eva.

And although she tried to convince herself that her reasons for wanting to leave Haiti were confined to the country's terrors, Claire had to admit she was not leaving Haiti only to protect Evan. She had escaped bomb threats, two hold-ups and several robberies and so far she had survived the ongoing uncertainty of being what she was christened the day of her wedding: Madame Dread, Georges's wife. Now, on her balcony in Key Biscayne, sipping good coffee, Claire laughed at the final danger that had sent her packing in less than two days, barely without thought. Gigi. The only good thing about Gigi was that she took away all of Claire's uncertainty: when Claire stormed out of her own house with Gigi's smell in her throat, the decision was mindless and pure.

Claire had came home unexpectedly from a job. The diplomat she was scheduled to interview in a town a few hours away had been wounded and the situation made it too dangerous to remain. She got home very late, closed the door quietly and tiptoed around the house, so as not to wake anyone. The house had a strange unsettling smell. In the living room, Claire saw that Eva had fallen asleep in her clothes on the couch; there was an open book on her stomach and an unfinished pork sandwich on the couch under her chin. Taking away the sandwich and the book, Claire covered her step-daughter with a light blanket and kissed the top of her head.

Evan was in his bed, naked and shivering in his sleep; she could smell that he had wet the bed. Carefully, she removed the soiled sheets, wiped him down with a wet towel, and wrapped him in a cotton blanket. Then she covered him with a larger quilt and went to her room, to find Georges. Just in front of the door, she smelled the smell she couldn't identify when she'd first walked

Diane Goodman

in. It wasn't Eva's body odor, which she knew well by now, and it wasn't her stale pork sandwich, either. The smell of her son's urine did not repulse Claire at all, but this smell made her gag.

"Georges," she exclaimed, opening the door, "what is that smell?" and just then she saw him wound around a naked, sweating Gigi.

"Wait," he'd said, but she was already halfway down the hall.

She gathered the slumbering Evan to the sound of her husband's pathetic pleadings, and left the house she owned to go to Candace's. There, she called her mother and said she and Evan would be moving to Key Biscayne; they needed the family condo down there for an indefinite period of time. Of course, her mother had said, and Claire had detected relief in her mother's voice. When are you coming? her mother had asked. Two days, Claire said with complete surety: we will be there in two days.

Over those two days, Georges followed her around the house as she packed, trying to convince her that sleeping with Gigi meant nothing. She ignored him. In his frustration, he tried to turn the blame to Claire: "You were away," he said.

"You're away every night at the club. You hardly ever sleep at home. I don't cheat on you."

"You went away," he said, again, as if she didn't get it the first time. "We need you."

"I was working. If I don't work, we don't eat. And you...you work all night long and bring home nothing. We don't need you."

She had a twinge of regret after saying that since it wasn't exactly true: they lived off her inheritance; she had willingly—happily—supported his career, financially and spiritually, because she believed in him; she worked because she loved it. But the rest was true. He was out all night; he brought home no money. He couldn't take care of his kids, not even for one night. He screwed that slut Gigi in Claire's bed. Who needed him?

But Georges was not ready to give up. When all else

184

failed, he blamed Gigi. She got him drunk; she followed him home; she told him Claire was cheating on him. He shouted all of this on the last day, while Claire packed Evan's things; hers were already in boxes, ready to be shipped.

"She seduced me. What was I supposed to do?"

You were supposed to say no, Claire thought. You were supposed to make the eleven-year old Eva take a bath, get into pajamas, put her unfinished sandwich into the cooler and get into bed. You were supposed to bathe your little son, put some nightclothes on him, read him a story, make sure he peed, sing him to sleep. You're a goddamned singer, for God's sake: you were supposed to sing him to sleep. Then you were supposed to get into our bed by yourself and try to fall asleep. You were supposed to miss me.

But Claire said nothing except that she was leaving and taking Evan with her. Then Georges broke down. He was a child who could not be consoled. He had tried every tactic he could think of to make Claire stay but nothing worked. Finally, he hit on something he knew would give her pause: how could she leave Eva? Eva, whose mother was a drug addict and barely remembered she'd had daughter; Eva who had been sent away to live with family friends at two years old and came back bone thin, unable to walk or make any sounds. During the first two weeks she was home, little Eva did not open her eyes. Certainly, she had suffered unthinkable kinds of abuse, but no one, especially not Eva, was talking.

In Claire's lap, Eva learned what it meant to be warm. Claire turned down two month's worth of work to lure Eva back to the world. She rubbed creams over the sores on Eva's back and neck; she fed her homemade broth, sang to her, told her stories and kissed her eyelids until they lifted on their own. Under Claire's care, Eva fattened and thrived. She started to sing. Eventually, she began to talk and ultimately, she learned to love to read.

"Fine, I'll take Eva, too." For Claire, it was a decision

made to win an argument—she hadn't really thought about what it meant; for Georges, it was neither a win nor a loss, but it was better than he expected: if Claire took Evan and Eva, she could never fully sever her bond with him.

So Claire had taken the children and come to Miami, to Key Biscayne. Her anger and her hurt, which pounded on her relentlessly from the moment she walked out of the house, had put her and her children on a plane and into her mother's condominium in two days. She was lonely, yes: not just for the Georges her mind had recreated, the early devoted Georges without faults or lies, but also for Candace, her community, the man she bought her tomatoes and peppers from, the old woman who painstakingly took in her skirts as she lost more and more weight, the next door neighbor who she trusted to care for her kids when she got called out to an assignment while Georges was playing music in the club. In Key Biscayne, although she knew how to operate on American soil, she knew no one: here, she was a stranger in the condominium she'd spent winters in as a child. And although she was free in ways she had forgotten about in Haiti—in Key Biscayne, she could go wherever she wanted, neglect to lock her doors, walk the beach at night—she felt like a prisoner: she was trapped with her children constantly and had no idea how to make friends.

In Haiti, although Georges refused to speak to Gigi ever again, he was forced to move into the house where she lived because he had nowhere else to go. He blamed Gigi for ruining his life and the way he hurt her was worse punishment than Claire, in her most vicious fantasies, could have imagined. But now Gigi was getting her revenge: *Georges's at Alta's.*

"Evan's in my bed." Eva came out onto the balcony and slumped down into the chair next to Claire. She opened her mouth and released a huge yawn. Claire could smell Eva's rank breath, not just from sleep but because Eva didn't pay attention to being clean. "He's sleeping there."

"So?" Claire sipped her coffee. Be calm, she told herself.

"It's my bed. What's he doing in there?"

"It's not your bed, Eva, it's mine: all of the beds are mine and Evan can sleep in any one of them." For a second, Claire felt justified—she owned everything this child had—but then she thought, Shit: what am I doing? It was hard to remember that Eva was only twelve.

But it didn't matter. "Sorry, Mom" was all Eva said, with the flat affect that characterized her. She yawned again.

"Eva, go brush your teeth."

"Okay, Mom," Eva said, but she sat there still.

"Go. Now."

"OK, Mom." And she got up. But instead of going into her bathroom, she went into the kitchen and began rifling through the cereal cupboard. "Do we have Fruit Loops, Mom?"

Eva tacked "Mom" onto nearly everything she said, as if she thought it was enough to keep Claire from abandoning her. In fact, it seemed to Claire that it was the only concession Eva made to making their life together easier, more meaningful. Eva seemed to be playing a part. She heard what Claire said and always responded as if she understood; but then she would do anything other than what Claire requested and, yet, without any obvious sense of her own disobedience.

Claire tried to be sensitive, to remember always what Eva must have suffered but never spoke of, to recognize how different the States were than Haiti; if it was hard for Claire to adapt to the place where she grew up, what must this be like for Eva? But things *were* different here—so much better and easier in so many ways—and, gently, Claire would try to teach Eva how to live like an American girl. Patiently, she explained to Eva that she could not continually misplace her books, her lunch money, her house keys, her bike lock. Yet nearly every day, Eva came home without something. Despite the conflicted feelings Claire had for Eva—loving her one minute, irrationally blaming her for her father's faults the next, becoming infuriated with her step-daughter's inability to fulfill a single simple request (put your cereal bowl in the sink, put your dirty clothes in the hamper), loving her again when Eva came out of her room to read Claire a passage she loved from a book—she managed somehow to balance her patience with her fury when it came to Eva's easy distraction and apparent lack of concern for the rules of daily life.

But Claire was not able to be so balanced about Eva's room and her hygiene: her room smelled like mold, stale milk, soured meat. They lived in a beautiful place on Key Biscayne but Eva smelled like the homeless who huddled on their corner in Haiti. Her bathroom was stained with urine, feces, menstrual blood. Claire couldn't bear to clean it and even after screaming at her, Eva didn't. She would say she would—"OK, Mom,"—but then ultimately Claire would pay the cleaning service extra to go in there. She'd also apologize.

Yet, it wasn't as if Eva took pleasure in defying Claire; it was more as though she thought that by merely agreeing, merely saying OK, that she was doing what was asked of her. She wasn't confused or scatterbrained; she was indifferent. She seemed to understand but not to care and that was one of the things that made it so difficult to remember that Eva was a child, a sixth grader. That and the fact that she looked like a grown woman.

By the time Eva was three, she had become by most accounts a normal child. She was curious, energetic, cute. She could play quietly and throw tantrums. But one thing Eva never developed was affection. The child bristled when hugged, had to be coaxed and bribed into goodnight kisses. Claire knew that Eva had suffered severely before finally coming home at two: no one knew exactly what had happened to her when she was sent away but whatever she had been through had produced her flat affect and detachment. No matter what Claire did, Eva's emotional hollow never filled in. And since they had been in the States, Claire had tried to mother Eva as best she could: they read together, played board games and rented movies to watch on TV. But Claire no longer cooked and Eva loved to eat; Claire loved sports and Eva hated being outdoors in the heat. Claire was clean, efficient and organized; Eva was unconcerned and indifferent and never planned ahead. Being the adult, Claire tried to compromise: she found frozen pizzas she could heat up and a store that sold already prepared chicken wings. She took Eva and Evan out for burgers and fries and sat there with a club soda while they gorged. But still, nothing changed; during rare moments when Claire felt warmth for her step-child, she would reach out to hug her and Eva would slip away.

"I want Fruit Loops too," Evan was coming out of Eva's room. He walked into the kitchen and put his arms around his sister's thighs.

"Get off me, you little nerd" she said, with real love and kindness. "We don't have Fruit Loops. How about Corn Flakes?"

"Sure," he said, and sat down on the floor. Claire studied him, her little son who had hurt her without knowing it, who she had hurt, who was too young to be sorry or to understand her pain. He wasn't fully awake and probably hadn't been earlier that morning; he waved at his mom and blew her a kiss. Small favors: he didn't remember that half an hour ago, he'd hated her.

Claire left the kids in the kitchen to battle about cereal and went back into her room. She closed the door. It was hard to be on your own raising two kids, especially one who is not your own, who you often don't even like. She felt scared and frustrated but somehow her dilemma made sense. In Haiti, she was not required to raise her children the way she had been raised and that was a good thing since she really didn't know how. It was so much easier to let them eat when they were hungry, to leave them with neighbors when she had to be away, to stay up all night with them eating grapes and sunflower seeds when she was home. But now that she was back in the States, in the condo of her childhood with all the memories of her warm, safe mother, all she wanted for Eva and Evan and for herself was what she remembered from her own childhood as a normal life. She wanted to take them to the playground; she wanted to make them meals and play scrabble. They should have slumber parties, get regular haircuts, go to reading night at the library, see a dentist. In Haiti, she was free of all these traditions; now, she wanted them back but didn't know how to get them. And while she was struggling to figure out how to raise both of Georges's kids in the safe way she remembered, and while he was still swearing he would do anything to get her back, he was screwing Alta.

She couldn't help it that the kids were up now: she had to call Georges before she had a chance to talk herself out of it. She dialed again.

"Hello."

"Gigi, this is Claire. Who's Alta?"

"Who?"

"You heard me, goddammit, Who the hell is Alta?"

"Alta? What do you mean, Alta?"

"I want her phone number now, Gigi, and I'm not fucking around."

"Not Fucking around? Hmm, too bad for you, sister. Well, Alta doesn't have no telephone number."

"Cut the shit, Gigi: give me her number."

"She doesn't have a number cause she doesn't have no phone." Claire could her Gigi laughing.

"I want to talk to Alta. Today. You tell me how."

"I don't know what you're talking about. You're crazy. What do you mean you wanna talk to *Alta*?"

"You said Georges was at Alta's."

"Yeah, you crazy-ass woman: Alta's, the coffee on the corner. He's back now. Here." Claire heard her handing over the receiver.

"Yeah?" It was Georges, his early morning voice. He didn't know who was on the other end of the phone; Gigi hadn't told him—she was still having some fun. It was a good trick.

"But you can't eat them all," Claire heard Eva say through her closed door, though she could tell they were on their way to her room.

"Why not?" Evan asked, "you do."

"Mom?" Eva came in first, trailed by her brother. On the other end of the line, Georges was swallowing coffee and then saying "hello?"

"Mom, can I go to the store? There's not enough Corn Flakes," Eva explained.

"And can she get Fruit Loops? Can I go?" Evan was leaning on Eva's long legs.

Claire looked at her kids. They were both still in their pajamas and although awake and hungry, their eyes showed the soft sweet puffs of sleep. It was Saturday morning and it was still early; but their cartoons were already on. She pulled her mouth away from the receiver and said to the kids, "Hey, you guys: go get dressed."

"Can I go to the store, Mom?" Eva asked again. Eva often went to the store when Claire couldn't or wouldn't.

"Yeah, can I, Mom?" Evan echoed.

"We're all going," Claire said, standing up. "Go get dressed. We'll go the store and get cereal."

When Claire was little, her mother used to take her to the grocery store and let her pick out cereal. Then she would cut up half a banana in semi-circles on top and Claire would eat all of the cereal first, save the bananas for last.

"And bananas," she said.

Claire could hear Georges still saying "hello?" on the other end of the phone but her plan was interrupted by another memory, one she had not thought of for many years. "And we'll buy some things so I can make you a surprise for lunch."

"You're gonna cook, Mom?" Eva asked.

"You're gonna cook, Mom?" her little brother echoed.

"Sort of," Claire said, "now go. Hurry up and get dressed."

Then into the phone she said, "Georges, it's Claire: I cancelled your tickets." She hung up and turned off the ringer on the phone.

Slipping off her nightgown and putting on some shorts

Diane Goodman

and a t-shirt, Claire tried to remember all she would need at the store. Her mother was an artist; she made huge abstract paintings in deep colors and they covered the high white walls in the huge house where Claire grew up. But despite her work, Claire's mother's full attention went into raising her daughter.

At the grocery store, Claire did not rush through the aisles as she normally did. Instead, she let the kids pick out cereals and snacks and drinks while she chose the ingredients for the special lunch her mother would make on Fridays for her and her best friend Debbie during grade school. They were the Little Lunch People. Their heads were Ritz Crackers, or slices of hard-boiled egg. For eyes they had raisins or slices of green olives or sometimes chocolate chips; the mouths were made of cucumber moons and Claire didn't think they had any noses. But they had clothes made out of triangles of Kraft Singles, spoonfuls of shaped peanut butter, circles of bread cut from the bottoms of jelly jars, squares of salami. Their arms and legs were celery sticks and for hair, her mom had grated curls of carrots. Around the plate were clouds made of blueberries, marshmallow and chocolate chip flowers, mountains of roasted peanuts, tiny pickle sticks for grass, bits of chopped tomato like red rain. Nothing went together. But when you ate away anything on your plate, you could immediately put it all back together again. There were bowls of everything already cut up and within seconds, you could replace or recreate anything that you thought your greed or hunger had taken away.

Gina

...But the argument is that from what is you cannot draw any information as to how you ought to act. And the transition from "is" to "ought" is usually called the naturalistic fallacy. I do not accept this..."Ought" is dictated by "is" in the actual inquiry for knowledge. Knowledge cannot be gained unless you behave in certain ways.

Jacob Bronowski, The Origins of Knowledge and Imagination (Law and Individual Responsibility)

Yesterday at work I could of got shot. And I'll tell you something, if I had been the customer instead of the cashier, I probably would of got shot. I might even be dead. But at least I would of stuck up for myself.

Check-out Aisle Six is mine at Costco and things usually go pretty smooth there, as checking out goes. There's a routine. I ask for the Costco Card if the customer isn't already pushing it in my face, slide the items across my scanner and put them right into the cart (we don't have bags at Costco because we don't need them; we're like a warehouse and most of our stuff wouldn't fit in bags, anyway) and then I say, "How will you be paying?" There are only three ways to pay at Costco: cash, cash card or American Express. We don't take other kinds of credit cards and we definitely do not take checks.

Customers pay and go. That's the way it is. Sometimes people joke around with me, which is fine as long as it's not too annoying or personal. Like when this one guy looked at my nametag and said, "Gina. What exactly does Costco mean?"

"I don't know, sir," I said politely even though I was thinking, who cares? You got your thirty-six rolls of toilet paper for twelve bucks. Jesus. I hate when people try to be clever.

"It means you get everything at cost," the woman behind him said. A real braniac, she was. Him, too, I guess.

"I know *that*," he said, kinda pissed off, and I thought they were going to get into it so I just rang up his toilet paper, case of wine and lawn chairs real fast and got him the hell out of there. Most people don't understand that there's more to being a cashier at Costco than just ringing up the junk people buy.

But that wasn't the scene where I thought I was going to get shot. That happened yesterday.

Saturday, really busy as usual on Saturday, and almost time for my break so I was trying to get these people out of my line. You can't go on a break at Costco if you've got people in your line, even if it is your time and your turn. I was dying for a smoke and the rest of my sandwich from lunch so I was moving. There were only three people in my line, four in Giselle's, Checkout Aisle Five. But there was also this big guy moving his cart back and forth between my aisle and Giselle's. He only had a tennis racket and a gym bag in his cart and he must have been in a hurry because he kept on trying to figure out which lane would be fastest.

Sometimes Giselle and me play a trick: we go real slow and try to see who can stall customers the longest. It's not that nice a thing to do but customers get good deals at Costco so the least they can do is wait. Giselle gave me the "let's stall" look but I was starving and wanting a smoke real bad so I shook my head "no" and moved this old woman with her case of tomato sauce through fast. She reminded me of Carolyn Petroni's grandmother who used to stand at their stove all day stirring sauce and frying sausage. She took care of Carolyn's baby while we were at school and kept the baby in a soup pot, tilted sideways on the kitchen floor. He was a small one. This old customer smelled like Carolyn's grandmother's onions, too. I was glad to get her out of there.

Then I had a guy with a set of blue plastic dishes (pretty nice) and some hot dogs, buns and chips (obviously on his way to a picnic) and then behind him, your typical mother whose kids are at camp: she had a cartload of kid food, you know—like pudding cups and juice boxes and those lunchable things where the meat and cheese come in little sections and don't need refrigeration: God, if I ever have kids, I swear I'll never feed them crap like that. Then she had some wine, probably for her and the hubby, tomato sauce, soup, and some other junk I can't remember.

Why me? I was thinking. I was giving the picnic guy back his copy of the receipt when the next thing I know, the big guy with the tennis racquet and gym bag just cuts in front of the lady with all the shit in her cart. I guess Giselle was playing the "let's stall" game without me because she still had three customers to my one and a half, until this guy pushed in.

As soon as picnic guy wheeled his cart away, tennis guy was shoving his Costco Card in my face. I looked at the woman behind him because I thought she should say something—I mean, this guy cut right in front of her—but she was staring down into her cart. So I just stopped in my tracks.

"Hey," I said, "she was first" so he turned to look at her but she wouldn't look up at him.

This dude was really big, he was like seven feet tall or something. And he was wearing one of those sleeveless under-shirts that some people call "wife beaters." You could see the hair coming out under his arms and it was gross. Speaking of his arms, which were more fat than muscular, they were covered with tattoos. I didn't want to stare but one tattoo was of a dragon, I think. I could see some flames. He didn't really look like the kind of guy who played tennis; maybe the racket and the bag were a present for someone. Anyway, I just stood there waiting for him to move because the lady was first but he didn't move. So I said it again.

"She was in line before you," is what I said and the big tattooed guy looked back at her again and I looked at her, too: come on, lady, stand up for your rights. She was around my Aunt Sissy's age, like maybe 29, and she had on beige shorts that were too tight for her, a pearl necklace and a pink sleeveless tank. You know, some people just shouldn't wear sleeveless and I had two of them in my line.

Then tattoo guy took a big breath, which puffed him all up like a chicken, and he looked down at me (since he was so tall) and said, "here" pushing the card in my face again.

Now I don't care for that. No, sir. I already knew this guy was a rude one since he'd cut in line but that was no excuse for being nasty to me. So I said, "what about the lady?" and just then she said in this high squeaky voice that didn't fit with her looks at all, "No, no, it's OK: let him go first," but she was still looking down at her cart full of junk and her face was turning all red.

"It's not OK," I said and to tell you the truth, I don't know what came over me. I mean, I was starving and I could taste the cigarette I really wanted to smoke but this guy was just going too far.

"You need to let her go first, sir," I said. At Costco, they like it if you call customers "maam" or "sir" (though sometimes it's kinda hard to tell) and then he slammed his fist down on my counter. Just slammed it down.

"Please," the lady said, "just let him go, ok? Just ring his items up first, I don't mind, I have time" and I swear I thought she was going to cry so even though I did mind, what could I do? I took his card, rang up the racquet and the bag that came to $62.79 and said, "How will you be paying?" in my most annoyed voice because I was feeling very annoyed

"Master Card," he said.

"We don't take that."

"What?" he said.

"We don't take Master Card, sir," I said, and I was really snotty.

"What do you mean you don't take Master Card?" he said.

"I mean we don't take that card." Geez. What's so hard to understand about that? Then he let out this big sigh, like *I* was bothering *him*, and pulled his wallet out of his fat butt. He ripped a check out of the wallet and filled it out.

"Here," he said, and shoved the personal check in my face.

"We don't take that neither," I said. I was getting mad.

So was he: he pounded his big fist on my counter again, looked around the store and then said, "why not?"

"I don't know why not," I said.

"Damn it," he said and I almost said, hey watch it, pal, but then he said, "then take the card. I got to go."

I sighed. You're supposed to know the rules of Costco; it's part of why you shop here.

"We take cash, cash cards or AmEx," I said.

"Yeah? Well, I ain't got those, Lady; I have Master Card or a check. So what'll it be?"

I hate it when people call me Lady. It's fine for other people, older people, but not for me.

So I got some pleasure out of saying, "Sorry, but we don't take those."

But I wasn't really sorry; I was glad to turn this jerk down. He started to look around again and the lady behind him was just grabbing onto her cart with both her hands, which looked like they were turning blue but I could see she had a big diamond on one hand and I guess an emerald with diamonds on the other—something green and shiny. I was looking at that ring trying to see if it was real but then I saw out of the corner of my eye the guy put his hand in his pocket and turn back to me and I swear I thought he was going to pull out a gun. I think the lady thought so too because she sucked a big gulp of air in and let out some noise, like a cry or something. I was thinking *what the hell?* in my head and then I got so pissed off because this guy was wasting my break and this lady wouldn't stick up for herself so I stood straight up and stared him down: go ahead, I thought, just pull a gun on me and see what happens.

Nothing happened for a while; it probably only took a few seconds but it seemed like a while. The guy stood there with his hand in his pocket, staring back down at me as if I was going to all of a sudden tell him we just decided to take Master Card—just for him—and the woman was sort of mumbling something in this really high voice; I thought I heard her say "God" and maybe she was praying but I was definitely praying he'd pull out a goddamn gun because I knew guys like this and I wasn't going to back down for nothing. Guys like this guy thought the rules weren't made for them because they were big and had enough balls to let some dude cut them for tattoos.

Go ahead, I thought, *try and shoot me.*

"What?" he said, although I hadn't actually said anything.

"Go ahead" I said, "I don't care. We don't take that card or checks and she," then I pointed to the woman, "was in line first."

"No," the woman said, louder this time, and I was saying "No, what? You were in line before him, for God's sake," when I braced myself to be shot because the guy was taking his hand out of his pocket. But then I saw he was only holding a load of crumpled up bills.

I knew that I probably had known the whole time he didn't have a gun. I heard the woman let out a big breath but I was watching the guy pull the bills apart and even I could see there was only a ten and some ones so he said "Shit" and then he pushed the cart with the racquet and the bag out into the exit area so hard it knocked into the popcorn stand behind my aisle. I heard a couple people yelling "Hey" and then I heard him say some worse cuss words that I am not about to repeat and he took off.

Once she saw he was really out of the store, the lady started to put her items on my ramp. Her face was bright red.

"You shouldn't have let him cut in front of you like that," I said to her because if she had stuck up for her rights, I'd be puffing away out behind the store right now. "I wouldn't of."

She didn't answer, just kept putting the things she wanted to buy on my conveyor. So I said it again.

"Well, you never know with people," she said, in this funny high voice, almost like she was singing, while she put a big flat of pudding cups on my ramp; she definitely had little kids; at least I hoped so. "You never know what people like that could do" and then she called me *dear*.

"Yeah," I said, taking her card because she had it out already and thinking that being called *dear* is even worse than *lady*, "but you know what? You don't know what people like me could do if they got mad enough and I'm pretty mad. Why didn't you say something? You were just going to let him cut in front of you as if you don't count? As if his stupid tennis racquet was more important than your kids' pudding?"

I had her Costco card in my hand but I hadn't swiped it through yet; I wanted an answer and I have a lot of patience if I am waiting for something I want.

"Well, he seemed to be in a hurry and I'm not?" she said, as if it was a question I was supposed to answer. How the hell should I know how much time she had.

"But what about the fairness, lady?" I said and I liked calling her lady. "What about the part where what he did was wrong?"

"Sometimes life isn't fair, dear," she said, as if she was my grandmother and as if that wasn't bad enough, she sighed and reminded me of teachers in high school when I gave the wrong answer: I wanted to punch her. "He seemed angry and so I felt it was best just to let him go."

"But what about me? I stuck up for you and you didn't say anything." She started looking around then, like maybe she thought someone was going to come and help her get out of this fight with me. But I knew no one would come so I said, "why? Just tell me why you didn't say anything."

She put her head down then and said, "I thought he might have a gun."

"If that guy had pulled out a gun," I said, loud, "and shot me, or you, we could of sued him and he would of gone to jail. Now he's out there and he's probably gonna do the same thing to someone else, right? It's not fair and it's your fault."

She looked up at me like I was crazy, so I said "What?"

but she didn't answer. I'm not crazy, I'm right: if someone cuts in front of you, you have every right to say something and if the guy who cuts in front of you gets pissed and hits you or pulls out a gun or something, you're even more right. And we have security guards all over Costco. What was the matter with her, anyway?

"How will you be paying?" I asked, and I almost said *dear* but she was already giving me her AmEx card. She wouldn't look at me but I was staring at her and I could see her face was still red. Ashamed, I said to myself, and she should be: what she did was wrong. I put her in her place, though; at least that was something. When I handed her the receipt to sign, she was shaking her head and I was gonna say, *hey, lady, what the hell do you have to shake you head about?* but just then a guy tried to get in line behind her with a warehouse cart full of office furniture.

"I'm closed, sir" I said, "why don't you try Aisle Five" and I gave Giselle this "gotcha" smile, though I knew she wouldn't care because it was almost five and she got to go home today at six anyways whereas I had to stay until 9:00 but I only had about eleven minutes for my break and I wasn't about to spend it ringing up swivel chairs and computer tables.

By the time I got to the break room, I only had about seven minutes left but I wasn't even hungry anymore so I just went out back to smoke. There were only two left in my pack and I was mad enough to smoke them both in that seven minutes so I'd have to tell Giselle to leave me a couple before she went home. I had a thought to go around to the front parking lot and talk to that lady again; I knew she'd still be at her car, piling in the puddings and juices and wine. Sure she was scared but I stuck my neck out for her; she owed me something, didn't she? I stood my ground, looked that asshole right in the eye and said, "she was here before you." She was there and he didn't even have cash or American Express. But she just let him walk all over us.

I lit the second cigarette from the first one and inhaled a huge drag. I took another big drag and then the cigarette got too hot and I was pissed that I'd have to wait a few seconds before taking another hit. I only had three minutes left. People don't get it. And you really know that at Costco. All these people who shop here can probably afford to buy a Costco but they come in here with their outfits and their jewelry and their American Express cards so they don't have to pay too much for boxes of spaghetti or dishwashing liquid. They look down at you all the time, like they're better than you because here they are buying all this useless shit and they're in a hurry and your job—your whole goddamned purpose for being in this world—is to hurry up and ring them up so they can go get their hair done and their nails polished and their BMWs washed. And then when they have a chance to do something right, they blow it. She had a chance to make that right: she was there first. And you know that if I thought that guy was gross, she probably wanted to faint. I have to deal with guys like that all the time when Giselle and I go out but she's probably never really seen a guy like that up close; and a guy like that? Well he deserved to be told where to go by a lady like her. What the hell did she know anyway? She probably never had to look at someone's gross underarm hair or smell their disgusting breath or tell them to fuck off because you just want to drink your drink and talk to your friend and not be hassled. No, she and her hubby probably stay home and watch HBO or take their fat little kids to miniature golf or get a babysitter and go to the country club and dance. Guys like that guy can't even get jobs at the country club; they probably don't even pump her gas or fix her toilet. The don't grab her ass when she's walking out of a bar or laugh in her face when they bump into her table and spill beer on her lap.

And I know something else she doesn't know: guys like that are afraid of rich people like her; they don't take anything serious from someone like me. And I know it because they're the only kind of guys I ever deal with and I don't need them in my goddamn line at Costco.

Then I heard Glenn Cox, our supervisor, call to me from

the inside the break room: it was time for me to go back.

I turned my light back on in Aisle Six and saw two teenage girls coming toward me with a cart full of CDs, licorice, a twelve pack of gum, a flat of Diet Coke and something big in a box: CD Player? Video camera? It wouldn't be too long until I found out.

"Giselle," I yelled over to Aisle Five. I was still pretty mad.

"Yeah?" she said, waving her last customer away and eyeing the girls in my line. Bitches, she mouthed and I nodded.

"Leave me two butts when you go, will you?"

"Yeah. You want me to bring 'em to you before I go?"

"No, just leave 'em behind the radiator in the break room," I said.

"Sure," she said. "What time're you gonna be home?"

"Usual," I said to her over the blonde's head and then to the blonde I said, "Costco Card" as if she was the stupidest bitch in the world because she was in line at Costco and didn't have her card out and while she tried to get her hands in the pockets of her too tight shorts I heard Giselle say, "You wanna go out tonight?" and I said, "you bet your skinny ass I do" and the blonde shot a look up at me and I stared her straight in the eye and said, "What?"

Spirit

If under changing conditions of life organic beings present individual difference in almost every part of their structure, and this cannot be disputed; if there be, owing to their geometrical rate of increase, a severe struggle for life at some age, season, or year, and this certainly cannot be disputed; then, considering the infinite complexity of the relations of all organic beings to each other and to their conditions of life, causing an infinite diversity in structure, constitution, and habits, to be advantageous to them, it would be a most extraordinary fact if no variations had ever occurred useful to each being's own welfare, in the same manner as so many variations have occurred useful to man.

Charles Darwin, The Origin of Species

She is standing in front of me with the items she wants to purchase, a quarter pound of Alaskan King Crab legs (which isn't much) and a package of pork feet. The crab legs are wrapped in white paper and then plastic but I look at the price sticker and know what is inside; the pork feet are side by side on a green Styrofoam tray and covered in plastic which is torn: one peachy foot, with a visible nail, is partially exposed.

She is fingering the exposed foot, working it out from under the cellophane entirely, with her thumb. Her nails are long and ovaled, painted a frosty orange. Her hands are dirty and I can't tell if the sour smell is coming from her package or herself; she is layered in mismatched crumpled soiled clothing, inexplicable in the glamour that is Miami Beach and in its stunning September heat.

She thumbs the pork foot, sets the package down, and smells her thumb. Then she looks at me and, smiling, puts her thumb and forefinger together to her lips and blows a kiss out into the air between our faces, the European gesture that says these pork feet (once cooked, I presume) will be delicious.

I nod and smile, as if I already have this knowledge, and try to turn away casually, slightly ashamed of my discomfort but unable to part with it as well. Although she seems harmless, even sort of sweet, I cannot shrink the swell of my desire that she just pay and leave—in addition, the smell is consuming this hot store. Then she begins mumbling something in Spanish and since I do not want to know if she is talking to me, I pretend to be reading the tabloid headlines and see that Teletubby Stars are being invaded by Evil Spirits. Below the headline is a picture of four fat multi-colored creatures grinning. I reach for the tabloid but am immediately distracted by the woman because now she is rearranging my items—a bottle of wine, a can of coffee, two cherry yogurts—into a tighter formation than the one I created when I merely set them down. This, I assume, is a gesture of gratitude: instead of taking her place at the back of the long check-out line, she had walked around to the bagging space and edged her very ample body between a man in the process of buying a lot of groceries—potatoes, a Cuban bread, fresh peas, oranges, a pork roast, a pre-cooked chicken, ground beef, Ritz Crackers, sour cream, a kind of cheese I didn't recognize—and me. No one said anything when she did this but my face must have indicated that it was all right because she stopped and stood in front of me.

Six months ago I left my life, which included a man who was simultaneously amused by and uncomfortable with the way strangers would just start talking to me, with a kind of intimacy and familiarity he could not manage himself. I was never able to explain either phenomenon. Camping at the beach every summer, families on bikes would ride right into our campsite to ask me what I was cooking for supper. Last summer, twin ten-year old sisters whose names I never knew, came every night to sample chicken strips or steamed shrimp or chunks of roasted corn. At Sam's Wholesale Club, people would stop me in the aisles and ask if I had ever used this tomato sauce, read this book, if I would sit in this office chair and see if it felt comfortable. Once, in a diner in Vermont, a man in the booth next to us asked if he could taste my omelet to see if it was what he wanted. I let him.

Perhaps it was this ease I had among strangers that, ultimately, propelled me 1500 miles away, to Miami Beach. I was not conscious of whatever quality it was I possessed that made people feel comfortable talking to me but, somehow, strangers knew I would not turn away. I have an ordinary face but there must be some kind of welcome in it.

In Miami, the language in my face helped me feel at home quickly. The valets who park my car and watch me carry armloads of books inside call me Professor, not knowing that nickname is actually the last vestige of a career I gave up when I left Pennsylvania. Although much younger than I am and unable to communicate beyond the small amounts of English and Spanish we trade, they are sweet and oddly protective, observing that I am a woman who lives alone. The building's security guards, Estella and Angel, pat my shoulder or squeeze my elbow when I pass them in the lobby. The ease of these gestures is at once comforting and unsettling: nearly total strangers, these people talk to me and touch me with a kind of affection and trust that in my long relationship was not available.

And now this small, stout woman, with a multi-colored knit cap pulled all the way down around her forehead and ears, large pink-framed eyeglasses, and several layers of collected clothing takes one look at me and hears in my face, "Sure, cut in line. Come in here in front of me with your crab legs and pork feet: I will make this OK for you."

When she has rearranged my items, she sighs—tired?— and leans slightly and softly against me. I do not dare move though I am not sure why. She is wearing an apron that reminds me of the Jewish grandmothers from my childhood—scoop-necked, capped ruffled sleeves, big pockets, sporting a ridiculous print of kitchen utensils and clocks. She is wearing it almost as a jumper over a knee-length navy blue silk sheath, what my aunts would have called "a good dress." But hers is extremely old and has taken on the dull shine of expensive fabric that has thinned and weakened; wrapped part way around the apron is an Indian print cloth, the kind of thing my friends and I used as bedspreads in college. It comes to her feet, which are a very dark brown from sun and dirt, yet her unclipped toenails are painted a glossy yellow. She is wearing brown sandals dotted with silver sunbursts. Tucked under her arm is a blue umbrella with a carved wooden duck for a handle. In between two fingers, a brand new bankcard.

213

Like many people in Miami, she speaks only Spanish and like some other people in Miami, I speak only English so I don't say anything when I notice that she has not removed the sticker that proclaims, "Call this number to activate your card."

I had stopped here, at my neighborhood grocery store, reluctantly. It was Friday afternoon and my new career as a high school English teacher gave weekends at home a new meaning: I craved silence, a kind that had become unbearable before I moved here. In a whirl of revelation, impulsive decisions and unlikely coincidences, I left the privilege of the academy, a seven-year long relationship and a group of close friends and found myself in a job for which I was overqualified and a small studio with a huge view of the Atlantic Ocean.

Coming home on a Friday to a weekend without communication, save for people in the elevator, clerks in stores, the valets, is celebratory now in ways that the eternal weekends in Pennsylvania were full of hopelessness and despair. Although those weekends weren't exactly silent, there certainly was no communication taking place. I drank too much, slept a lot, and spent Saturday nights at the house my boyfriend clearly had built for himself, silently watching movies on the VCR. The next day, I couldn't remember what I had seen, my mind having left the film before it even started in search of the words that would reveal why we—two middle-aged people who claimed to love each other—could not discover what it was we needed and go on to make a life together. By the time I left, my every attempt—and there were many—at this conversation resulted in doors slamming, screaming, crying, cars screeching off, more wine, more sleep.

Now when I get home on a Friday evening, I change into sweats, pour a glass of wine, put on music and get into bed with a novel not because I have to but because I want to: I have a choice. The same actions in Pennsylvania were forced, pushed, necessary avenues of avoidance because I could not find a way to make solid my evaporating relationship, because the genuinely wonderful friends I had at the university looked forward to weekends with their spouses and children, because the small, impoverished town I lived in was inhospitable to who I hated to admit I had become: a woman utterly, indisputably, alone. On Miami Beach, I had the beach as a backyard, a neighborhood full of bookshops, theatres, outdoor cafes constantly filled with tables for one, an open air market selling flowers and fruit. I had a kind of courage that startled me each time I took myself to a movie, a concert, an expensive dinner. From my studio, I had a limitless view of the ocean. I had hope.

Unlike the life I had recently left, I could not wait to get home on the weekends. But this particular weekend, I was out of wine and coffee and I had recently returned to the real pleasure I naturally took in small things, like the feel of cold fruity yogurt in my throat. So I had stopped at the hot and crowded grocery store. And although I can't explain it, moving 1500 miles from home had also replaced the constant anxiety I battled there—in a place I knew well—with a kind of superior patience, in a place I did not know at all. I had done this, left an entire life and struck out on my own. I could sit by the window and wait for the rains to stop when I wanted to go to the beach. I could sing along with radio and wait for the traffic to begin to move on I-95. I could wait for another relationship, or not; after so many years driven by the compulsion to talk—the endless efforts to unearth what I now know were unknowable answers—I could spend my weekends in silence. I could wait for a more fulfilling career. I could wait for this old Cuban woman to buy her dinner.

But the woman running the cash register cannot wait and she is quickly becoming very impatient; the store is small, the line very long, and the old woman's bankcard will not register in the machine. The boy in line behind me, a beachy type with one of those absurd haircuts—shaved all around the ears, heavy mass of curls on top dyed sunshine yellow—sighs loudly. All he wants to buy is a can of Pringles, a Coke, and a package of red licorice.

"Your card," says the checkout woman, whose nametag reads Loretta, "isn't working."

"Si, si. Works," the old woman shouts. And then she smiles but not apologetically: she smiles as if she and Loretta are agreeing happily.

"No, no, doesn't work," mimics Loretta in a snappy voice, phony Spanish accent. "See?" and she swipes the bankcard back and forth very quickly through the machine, pointing to the blank screen where no information appears. "No work."

Lots of people here speak Spanish but no one wants to get involved.

"Works," exclaims the old woman and then she looks up at me. To help? To prove it?

"I wonder if she's called to activate the card," I offer, pointing to the white strip with toll-free number. "Did you call," I ask, putting a closed fist to my ear and cocking my head slightly to act out my question.

"Si, si," she says quickly.

"Oh come *on*," the boy behind me snorts and then pushes his junk food up against my items for emphasis.

"I'll have to punch the numbers in myself then," Loretta sighs. "I hate this. I really hate this," she says and the little woman nods her head up and down vigorously as if she understands and hates the punching in of numbers, too. She has one hand in the air and the other lays in such a way that her own orange thumb nail is side by side with the toe nail on the exposed pork foot. Then she lifts the package to her nose and takes a deep, exaggerated sniff, and the boy behind me cannot help but blurt out, "Oh for Christ's sake!"

Immediately, the old woman's head cranks back unnaturally far; her lips come apart to reveal brownish crooked teeth, a silent snarl. She pulls the pig foot easily from the cellophane and puts it in its entirety to her mouth, repeating the earlier kissing gesture but this time it is directed to the boy and it is not warm. Real fear darkens his face but he cannot look away from her. The phrase Evil Spirit occurs or recurs to me, pulls my glance around and down to her small round face, framed by the multi-colored winter hat. She winks.

The card will not register. Loretta tries the numbers three times but nothing happens. The small amount of crab legs and the package of pork feet come to a total of $7.71. So what happens next is not dramatic or romantic or heroic. I move the beachy boy's junk food away from my items and pull the crab legs and pork feet into them. I think about speaking but instead just nod at Loretta, who rings up all the items together and takes my money.

Now the old woman uses her big layered body to nudge the bag boy out of the way and begins to pack our groceries. She does not do this out of shame or gratitude; she does it out of solidarity. When she is done, she hands me my bag and walks out of the store while I am still waiting for my change.

By the time I get out of the store, she is just a few feet away from me and I have an urge to shout, to stop her and say something. But I don't. It's not because I don't know Spanish or because I do know that despite my newly discovered courage, starting up any kind of relationship with this woman is not smart—though both of these things are true. And it's also not because I have a sneaking suspicion that she may have put one of those pork feet in my bag and I want to return it to her because it is so precious. It is because, finally, I know with relief that there is nothing I need to say.

Acknowledgements

I am self-conscious about making an acknowledgements page that is longer than any of these stories and about sounding self-important and overly dramatic, but the fact is that there is a group of people who I blame for putting me in this dilemma because without them, I really never would have written this book.

Anonymously, two exceptional friends: one, who in the midst of all she is always doing, read every line of this entire book twice and with what can only be described as the most genuine wisdom I have ever encountered - as always, she gave me exactly what I needed; and my visionary friend who early on said to me, "you seem to be writing a book about women in grocery stores." And so I did.

My family, who read this as I wrote it and even in its early weaker stages said they were proud: I'm not good at saying how I feel but that meant everything: Dad & Judy, Mom & Alex, and my siblings - without whom I would be lost - Lee & Regina, Krissy and Jenny.

My friends: Beth D, with me in all things; dear Jen, who was invaluable in this as in everything; Maggie, who read the whole thing the minute I gave it to her, Cookie & Bill, for the birds in Louisiana and their ending; re-found Juan, assuring me this is not just a chick book; the wonderful Chris Browne and Sarah Stamler, and of course, always Laurel.

Diane Goodman
Miami, FL August 2001

Carnegie Mellon University Press
Series in Short Fiction

Very Much Like Desire
Diane Lefer

A Chapter from Her Upbringing
Ivy Goodman

Narrow Beams
Kate Myers Hanson

Now You Love Me
Liesel Litzenburger

Lily in the Desert
Annie Dawid

The Demon of Longing
Gail Gilliland